RISKED

← THE MISSING: BOOK 6 →
RISKED

MARGARET PETERSON
HADDIX

SIMON & SCHUSTER BOOKS FOR YOUNG READERS

NEW YORK LONDON TORONTO SYDNEY NEW DELHI

SIMON & SCHUSTER BOOKS FOR YOUNG READERS
An imprint of Simon & Schuster Children's Publishing Division
1230 Avenue of the Americas, New York, New York 10020

SIMON & SCHUSTER BOOKS FOR YOUNG READERS is a trademark of Simon & Schuster, Inc.
For information about special discounts for bulk purchases, please contact Simon & Schuster Special Sales
at 1-866-506-1949 or business@simonandschuster.com.
The Simon & Schuster Speakers Bureau can bring authors to your live event. For more information or to
book an event, contact the Simon & Schuster Speakers Bureau at 1-866-248-3049 or visit our website at
www.simonspeakers.com.
Book design by Drew Willis
The text for this book is set in Weiss.
Manufactured in the United States of America • 0713 FFG
2 4 6 8 10 9 7 5 3 1
Library of Congress Cataloging-in-Publication Data
Haddix, Margaret Peterson.
Risked / Margaret Peterson Haddix. — 1st ed.
p. cm. — (The missing ; bk. 6)
Summary: Jonah, thirteen, and Katherine, eleven, travel through time to 1918 Russia just as Alexei,
Anastasia, and the rest of Tsar Nicholas II's family is about to be executed.
Author's note includes facts about the Romanovs and the mystery surrounding their deaths.
ISBN 978-1-4169-8984-4 (hardcover : alk. paper)
ISBN 978-1-4424-2647-4 (eBook)
1. Nicholas II, Emperor of Russia, 1868–1918—Family—Fiction. [1. Time travel—Fiction.
2. Aleksei Nikolaevich, Czarevitch, son of Nicholas II, Emperor of Russia, 1904–1918—Fiction.
3. Anastasia, Grand Duchess, daughter of Nicholas II, Emperor of Russia, 1901–1918—Fiction.
4. Soviet Union—History—Revolution, 1917–1921—Fiction. 5. Science fiction.] I. Title.
PZ7.H1164Ris 2013
[Fic]—dc23
2012006770

FIRST
EDITION

For my parents, who told me fascinating stories
about Russia when I was a kid

RISKED

ONE

Jonah Skidmore took a deep breath as he peered at the computer screen in front of him. He'd recently survived time travel, a war zone, betrayal, deception, mutiny, and the near destruction of time itself. So surely he was brave enough to call up a list of names on a computer.

Wasn't he?

He kept his finger poised over the computer mouse.

I'll be brave enough in a minute, he told himself. *Or . . . two.*

"What's wrong?" his sister, Katherine, said from behind him. "Did Google lock up or something? Hit that link again."

Patience wasn't one of her virtues. Before Jonah had a chance to reply, she shoved her hand over his, pressing his finger down on the mouse.

"There," Katherine said. "Just what we need. Famous missing children in history. Let's see . . ."

There was a good chance that Jonah's name might be on the list coming up on the computer screen before them. Not his real name—not Jonah Skidmore. But his original name. The name he'd been born with.

To keep from actually looking at the screen now, Jonah whirled in his seat to glare at Katherine.

"Keep your voice down!" he commanded. "Do you want Mom or Dad to hear?"

Unfortunately for Jonah, his parents were the kind who believed all those warnings about monitoring kids' computer use. So the Skidmore family computer was right smack in the middle of the kitchen. And Mom and Dad were just around the corner and down the hall, where they were hanging Jonah's and Katherine's newest school pictures along the staircase.

Mom and Dad had no clue that Jonah and Katherine had traveled through time again and again and again, their lives in danger in one century after another.

But even without the complications of time travel and historical danger and intrigue, Jonah wouldn't have wanted his parents to know how desperate he was to find out his preadoption identity.

Not that I exactly want *to know it,* he told himself. *I just . . . need to.*

"Mom and Dad wouldn't mind us talking about history,"

Katherine said, barely bothering to lower her voice. Then she leaned in closer and dropped her voice to a total whisper: "Do you think you might be the Russian kid?"

She pointed to a name on the screen.

Jonah grimaced so fiercely he could barely see.

What if I'm wrong about everything? he wondered. *What if there's some chance my other identity will never actually matter? Can't I go on ignoring it and pretending it doesn't exist?*

He knew the answer to that question: No. He couldn't. He was only thirteen—and Katherine was not quite twelve—but in the last few months they'd learned that the past had a way of coming back and grabbing you.

Sometimes literally.

That is not the right way to think about time travel, Jonah told himself. *Remember, you have a new attitude now.*

He forced himself to open his eyes wide enough to read the words on the screen before him—and then wider still, in indignation.

"Alexis Romanov?" he protested. "No way—that's a girl's name!"

Katherine reached over Jonah's shoulder and clicked on a link for the name.

"No, it's a guy," she corrected. "It's Russian, remember? Sometimes he's listed as Alexis, sometimes Alexei. Same kid, just different translations. Definitely a boy. See?"

Phrases jumped out at Jonah from the screenful of information she'd called up: *heir to the throne of the Russian empire . . . World War I . . . Russian Revolution . . . Alexis was imprisoned with the rest of his family . . . then in 1918 the Bolsheviks decided . . .*

Jonah didn't know much about Russian history—or anything about it, actually—but he was pretty sure that things hadn't gone well for this Alexis or Alexei Romanov back in 1918.

Well, duh, Jonah told himself. *Kids don't vanish from history because everything's going great. All of us were in some kind of danger.*

For most of his life, Jonah had believed what his parents believed: that he was a perfectly ordinary kid in a perfectly ordinary family, growing up in a perfectly ordinary Ohio suburb. He was adopted and his sister wasn't—that was the only detail about him that had ever seemed the least bit unusual. And Jonah's attitude toward that little fact had always been, *Well, so what? Who cares?*

Then the mysterious letters had begun arriving, and Jonah had found out that he wasn't an ordinary adoptee.

Not at all.

Instead, he and thirty-five other kids were, depending on how you looked at it, either refugees from history or children audaciously stolen from the past. Or both at once.

The only reason he and the other kids were growing up now, at the start of the twenty-first century, was because their kidnappers had crash-landed in this time period with a planeload of stolen babies. Fearing the wrath of time agents determined to keep history on its original track, the kidnappers had abandoned the babies and run away, vowing to come back for them as soon as they could.

At least we got thirteen years of happy ignorance before everyone started fighting over us again, Jonah thought.

And that wasn't the right way to think either. Ignorance wasn't a good thing. Jonah and Katherine had traveled back and forth through history multiple times in the past few months, repairing time and rescuing other kids endangered by their own time periods. How many times on those trips had ignorance almost gotten someone killed?

Let's see . . . in 1483 . . . 1485 . . . 1600 . . . 1605 . . . 1611 . . . 1903 . . .

Jonah had returned from his last trip through time vowing to face up to even the facts he desperately *didn't* want to know.

Facts like what his original identity in history actually was.

Just yesterday he'd asked JB, the time agent he knew best, to finally reveal it.

This may have been a little unfair. After their last trip

through time, JB was going through an identity crisis of his own. It probably wasn't surprising that JB had refused to tell.

So Jonah had decided to take matters into his own hands.

Because you never know, Jonah told himself. *You never know when I might be zapped back in time, when I might have to deal with whatever historical mess this Alexis or Alexei Romanov—or whoever I really am—had to deal with. I refuse to take another time-travel trip blind!*

He made himself focus on the words on the screen and read them in order, not skipping around:

Alexis Romanov, the last tsarevitch of Russia, was born in 1904. He had four older sisters—Olga, Tatiana, Maria, and Anastasia—but as the first and only male child of Tsar Nicholas II, he was the designated heir, intended from birth to inherit the throne. At that time, the Russian empire covered a sixth of the globe . . .

Jonah stopped reading.

"If I really was, like, the future leader of Russia, don't you think I'd . . ." He let his voice trail off, because there was no way he could say what he was thinking. *If I really am this kid, shouldn't I feel more special? Shouldn't I be smarter, more* talented—*more obviously someone capable of ruling a sixth of the planet?*

"What? Do you think you should *look* more like a prince—or a 'tsarevitch' or whatever the Russians called it?" Katherine teased. "Do you think you shouldn't look like such a goofball?"

"How I should look . . . ," Jonah muttered. "Duh, Katherine, we're idiots. In 1918 they had cameras. They—"

He stopped explaining and started typing instead. He clicked back over to Google and started an image search for Alexis or Alexei Romanov.

Within seconds he'd called up a picture of a boy in a sailor suit. The kid was maybe nine or ten, and staring unsmilingly toward the camera. It was a black-and-white image, so it was impossible to tell if the boy's hair was brown or just dark blond. It was impossible to tell eye color. It was impossible to tell why the boy looked so serious. But Jonah could tell one thing for sure:

"It's not me," he said, relief swimming over him.

Katherine squinted at the picture.

"Maybe you just think that because it's such an old picture, and you're used to seeing yourself in this century," she said. "Or—you know how sometimes people don't look like themselves in one particular shot?"

Jonah clicked the back arrow, returning to the lineup of

dozens of images of Alexis/Alexei Romanov. He reached to the top of the computer desk, where Mom had stashed the packets of the other copies of his and Katherine's school pictures, ready to be handed out to various relatives at Thanksgiving. He shook out a five-by-seven of himself and held it up beside the computer screen.

"See?" he said. "No way that's me."

"Okay," Katherine said softly.

She was looking too closely at the picture of Jonah. Jonah couldn't help staring at it too.

Did anybody like his or her seventh-grade school picture? Jonah's hair stuck up in a weird way, and his grin was both crooked and too wide. But there was something else about the picture that bothered Jonah.

It was taken back in September, before I got the first letter. Before I went back in time for that first trip. It might as well have been a million years ago.

The Jonah in the picture looked too baby-faced, too unformed, too innocent.

Too ignorant.

It hurt, just looking at this picture of the kid Jonah had once been.

No wonder Katherine was doubtful about Jonah and Alexei/Alexis's appearance. Even Jonah didn't look like himself anymore.

He turned the picture facedown and slipped it back into the packet at the top of the computer desk. He caught only a glimpse of the packet of Katherine's school pictures, the multiple images of her blond hair, her blue eyes, and her confident gaze, which seemed to say, *You think there are going to be a lot of mean girls in sixth grade? So what? I'm not worried!*

As if that was all Katherine was ever going to have to worry about.

Katherine looked like a total little kid in her school pictures from a few months ago too.

"Oh, hey," he said loudly, trying to distract himself and Katherine. He pointed back toward the computer screen. "Why are all these pictures of girls mixed in with the images of the *boy* Alexis? Maybe you're wrong after all."

Katherine took control of the mouse and the keyboard again.

"No, those are his sisters," she said, clicking through images until she came to a large one of four girls in lacy white dresses and Alexis/Alexei—looking much younger—in yet another sailor suit. "Do you remember, back in the time cave, back in the beginning of all this, when we saw all the names of the missing kids from history on that plane? Two Romanovs were on that list, weren't they? Alexis and Anastasia?" She zoomed in until only the two youngest children showed on the screen. "Do these kids look familiar?"

Jonah frowned. He had met almost all of the other kids stolen from history in the time cave, the day the original kidnappers had come back hoping to retrieve each one of them. But Jonah didn't have quite enough imagination to mentally replace the old-fashioned lace dress and sailor suit in the picture of the Romanovs with the modern jeans and T-shirts and sweatshirts the other kids had been wearing in the time cave.

"I don't know," Jonah said irritably.

Anastasia and Alexis Romanov seemed to stare back at him from the computer screen, their expressions plaintive and pleading. Jonah wished he'd never thought to look for pictures. Now that he knew he himself wasn't a Romanov, he didn't want to learn anything else about these kids. It was too much of a burden. He already had to worry about his friends Chip and Alex, trying to recover from the trauma of the 1400s, and his friend Andrea, who'd wanted to stay in 1600 even though it was a complete mess, and Emily, who—

Katherine gasped beside him. Jonah turned and saw that she'd gone totally pale.

"What's wrong with you?" he muttered.

"Everyone's just supposed to be missing, right?"

Katherine asked, her voice shaking. "You and the other kids—you just vanished from history and nobody was ever supposed to know what happened to you. Isn't that how it was always supposed to be? For all thirty-six of you?"

"Uh, sure," Jonah said uneasily. "Why?"

Katherine raised a trembling hand and pointed to a sentence Jonah hadn't noticed before, directly below the picture on the screen.

"Because," Katherine said. "Because this says Anastasia and Alexis Romanov are dead."

TWO

Jonah read the sentence beside Katherine's fingertip:

> Thanks to this most recent DNA testing,
> we now know that the entire Romanov
> family was executed in the early morning
> hours of July 17, 1918.

"Did *we* do that?" Katherine asked in a strangled voice.

"I think we would have known if we'd killed anyone," Jonah said, trying to make a joke of things. He couldn't take Katherine sounding so grim. "Let alone *executed* a whole family. Besides, we've never even been to 1918."

"No, I mean, is it our fault?" Katherine asked. "Did something we changed in time on one of our trips make it so Alexis and Anastasia died in 1918 instead of being kidnapped and turned back into babies and brought to our time?"

Jonah had known that that was what she meant. He leaned his head back.

"JB?" he called softly. "Don't you think now would be a good time to show up and explain everything?"

This was a little twisted. Five minutes ago Jonah had been hoping that JB wouldn't know what he and Katherine were up to. Now Jonah *wanted* the time agent to be watching and listening and ready to swoop in.

Jonah looked around. He heard footsteps coming toward the kitchen.

And then Mom came around the corner, a hammer in one hand and a yardstick in the other.

"Every year," she said, shaking her head grimly. "Every year we *think* we're going to be able to hang those pictures without having them look crooked. And every year we find out we have to measure down from the ceiling, not up from the baseboard along the stairs . . . and it still drives us crazy trying to do it right. What are you two up to?"

Jonah could feel the guilty expression spreading over his face.

"Nothing," he said.

"School project," Katherine said.

Mom glanced at the computer screen.

"The Romanovs and the Russian Revolution?" she said, sounding surprised. "Which of you is studying that? Jonah, I thought your social studies class was working on the Minoans and the Mycenaeans. And Katherine, I thought you were still on that geography unit."

Sometimes it really stank to have parents who paid attention to what you were doing in school.

"It's kind of an extra-credit thing," Katherine lied smoothly. "You know Mrs. Hatchett thinks the curriculum leaves out a lot. She likes to add enrichment activities."

Jonah had to hand it to Katherine: She rolled her eyes so convincingly that even Jonah almost believed her.

"I was helping Katherine look up a few things," Jonah added, to explain why he was sitting in the computer chair and Katherine was standing beside him.

Katherine shot him a disgusted look, as if to say, *Now you're pushing it too far. That's just going to make Mom more suspicious! Why would I need your help?*

Mom leaned in toward the computer, staring at the picture of Alexis and Anastasia.

"Good for Mrs. Hatchett," she said absently. "It's great she's trying to make history come alive. . . . I remember being fascinated by the Anastasia story when I was about your age, Katherine. Of course, that was before they'd found any of the bones."

"Bones?" Jonah repeated faintly.

"Well, yeah—how much research have you done so far?" Mom asked.

"We just started," Katherine said.

Mom put down the hammer and yardstick and took over the keyboard and mouse.

"I'm trying to remember when everything was revealed," she said, starting new searches of her own. She clicked through one screen after another until she came to a list of dates. "Okay, here we go. This says the family was killed in 1918. At first the Soviet leaders said only the tsar had been executed, so there were all sorts of stories floating around about what had happened to the rest of the family. Somehow it was almost always the youngest daughter, Anastasia, that people thought had escaped—a woman showed up in Germany years later claiming to be her, and even some of the Romanov relatives believed her."

"Why Anastasia?" Jonah asked. "Why not one of the other girls? Or the boy?"

"I don't know," Mom said, tilting her head thoughtfully. "Maybe it was because Anastasia had a reputation for being feisty, and the other girls didn't. The son, though—he was so sick to begin with. . . . It was kind of amazing he lived as long as he did, anyway."

"He had hemophilia," Katherine said, sounding like

such an expert. Which was ridiculous, because Jonah knew she hadn't known that a moment ago. She was just reading from the computer screen.

"Right," Mom said.

"And there wasn't a cure for that back then, but there is now, right?" Katherine said. Jonah could tell she was trying to catch Jonah's eye without Mom noticing. At least one of the other missing children from history—Emily, the girl they'd helped most recently—had been endangered in her original life by an illness.

But Mom was frowning.

"I'm not sure there's a cure for hemophilia even now," she said. "But I'm pretty sure it's treatable. We can look that up too—"

Jonah didn't have the patience for a long detour. He put his hand protectively over the mouse.

"Katherine can do that later," he said. "Keep explaining—what were you saying about bones?"

"Well, the rumors kept flying for decades, because the people who murdered the Romanovs hid the bodies," Mom said. She pointed to a chunk of text on the screen. "It was about sixty years before anyone found any of them, and—look here—even that was kept secret until 1989, about the time the Soviet Union was starting to fall apart. There were tests done on the bones after that, and scientists said it was the tsar, his wife, three of the daughters, the family's doctor, and three loyal servants. The bodies of the son and one of the daughters were missing."

"So Anastasia and Alexis could have escaped!" Jonah exclaimed. "The fact that their bones weren't with the rest of the family's—isn't that kind of proof that they did?"

Mom was scanning the computer screen.

"Well, there was some disagreement about whether it was Anastasia or Maria whose bones were missing," she said. "And anyhow—here it is—in 2007 someone found other bones nearby, and they did DNA tests and then the scientists pretty much said, 'It's a hundred percent certain. These are the missing Romanov bones. The whole family died in 1918. No one escaped.' Tragic, isn't it?"

Now Jonah was the one trying to catch Katherine's eye. The year 2007 wasn't that long ago. If he and Katherine had changed something in history that led to the death of Anastasia and Alexis Romanov in 1918, wouldn't time agents like JB have tried to keep it secret as long as they could?

Would JB have even bothered to tell Jonah and Katherine what had happened?

Was there any way to undo whatever had changed Anastasia's and Alexis's fates?

"JB, we *really* need an explanation," Jonah muttered,

softly enough that there was no way Mom could hear.

The doorbell rang just then, and the sound made Jonah jump.

"I'll get it," he said, sliding out of the chair.

If that's JB—wow, that was quick, he thought.

He just needed to be prepared to play along with whatever story JB would come up with to explain his presence to Jonah's parents.

Jonah rushed down the hall and yanked the door open.

It wasn't JB. But it was someone Jonah recognized.

There, on the Skidmores' porch, stood Anastasia Romanov.

THREE

To his credit, Jonah did not blurt out, *Aren't you supposed to be dead?*

He did consider it. His mind tried out and discarded several other possible things to say, but most of them sputtered away after an initial *What . . . ? How . . . ? Why . . . ?*

Maybe you could figure out a few things before you say anything, he told himself.

He blinked a few times, and his eyes kept assuring him that this was the exact same Anastasia Romanov he'd seen on the computer screen only a moment earlier. She had the same rounded face, the same impish gleam in her eyes, the same long, flowing hair. But this wasn't like seeing a black-and-white picture colorized and come to life. The Anastasia standing before him wasn't wearing a strand of pearls around her neck. She didn't have her dark blond hair pulled back in some puffy old-fashioned style; it was parted on the side and tucked behind her ears. The long, lacy white dress from the picture had been replaced with blue jeans and a University of Michigan sweatshirt.

So it's not Anastasia zapped straight from the early 1900s to our front porch, Jonah thought. *It's modern Anastasia, Anastasia who's grown up in the late twentieth and early twenty-first centuries, just like me.*

So if Anastasia was standing on Jonah's front porch, why did the Internet say DNA tests proved she had died in 1918?

And if she was one of the kidnapped/time-crashed missing children from history, like Jonah, why didn't Jonah remember seeing her at the time cave when almost all of them had been gathered together? Especially since, now that he was looking right at her, he could tell that even in blue jeans and a sweatshirt Anastasia Romanov looked 100 percent like Anastasia Romanov?

Jonah realized that he'd been standing there for a ridiculously long time staring at Anastasia without saying anything. The only thing he'd done was blink and maybe open and close his mouth a few times like a fish.

"Okay, okay," Anastasia burst out. She crossed her arms defensively across her chest. "I get it that people in Ohio hate the University of Michigan, and I'm making everyone

I meet hate me by wearing this shirt. But *get over it*. All my other clothes are in boxes being carried off the moving van right now. I'll wear something different tomorrow. Sheesh."

University of Michigan, Jonah thought. The University of Michigan was in Michigan, of course. Jonah even knew what city it was in: Ann Arbor. And there was something important about Ann Arbor, Michigan, something that had to do with someone moving . . .

Jonah's brain couldn't quite make the shift from thinking about people moving from one time period to another, to thinking about people moving from one state to another.

He was still squinting stupidly at Anastasia when he noticed his friend Chip jogging up the sidewalk.

"Daniella insisted on meeting you," Chip said. "Posthaste."

Jonah frowned at Chip and shook his head warningly. Chip had been back from his trip to the 1400s for a couple of weeks now, but he still sometimes acted and sounded like he was stuck in the Middle Ages. He'd lived the years 1483 to 1485 as Edward V, an English king who'd mysteriously vanished from history. Jonah could see how it would be a little hard to just snap back into normal life. But Chip really needed to be more careful.

"Er . . . remember Daniella McCarthy?" Chip asked, trying to cover his mistake. He gestured toward Anastasia.

Evidently, Daniella was her twenty-first-century name. "Remember how I talked to her on the phone before she moved down here?"

That was the hint Jonah needed. It was a first step, anyhow. Way back when Chip and Jonah and Katherine were just starting to figure out that something very, very weird was going on, they'd come across two lists of names, one labeled "survivors" and one labeled "witnesses."

Daniella McCarthy's name, like Chip's and Jonah's, had been on the survivors list.

But is she actually a survivor if she's really Anastasia and the Internet says Anastasia Romanov died in 1918? Jonah wondered. *What sites were we looking at, anyway—would the school librarian say they weren't reliable?*

But if this was just a case of getting bad info from the Internet, why had Jonah's own mother been convinced that Anastasia was dead?

Jonah realized he was still staring stupidly at Daniella.

"Oh, uh, welcome to Ohio," he managed to say. "Your family's moving into your new house right now? To—" He barely stopped himself from saying, *To 1873 Robin's Egg Lane?* It would seem way too creepy and stalkerish that he remembered her street address. Especially if she didn't know . . .

Wait a minute, Jonah thought. *She doesn't know anything.*

Daniella McCarthy was the one and only missing kid from history who wasn't in the time cave that day we found out everything. Because there was some kind of mix-up that delayed her move. So she doesn't know she's in the wrong time period. She doesn't know people have been fighting over whether to take her back to the past or on to the future. She only knows what Chip told her when he called her on the phone, and that was before we knew much of anything ourselves.

Really, the only thing Chip had talked about with Daniella was her move. Not time travel. Not history. Not her identity.

Jonah cleared his throat, delaying.

"To . . . ," Daniella prompted him.

"To . . . Hey, wasn't there some problem with the paperwork for your house? Messing things up? Your parents must have worked it all out, huh?" Jonah asked. As soon as he said this, Jonah realized it was a mistake. He didn't have a good excuse for knowing about the paperwork problems.

"Everything worked out. Unfortunately," Daniella said, with an emphatic eye roll. "I still hate Ohio. And I hate my parents for making me move."

"It's not so bad here," Chip said quickly.

Jonah saw that both of them were just acting. Neither one of them actually wanted to talk about the pros and cons of moving to Ohio. Daniella's bright blue eyes darted about, studying first Jonah's face, then Chip's. She seemed to be waiting to see what they would accidentally reveal next. Chip was watching Daniella just as carefully, as if waiting for her to ask, *Whoa, dude. How is it that you even know about my parents' paperwork problems? And, while you're at it, would you mind explaining how you two yahoos knew about my move in the first place—before I did?*

Why didn't she just come out and ask? Didn't she trust them to give her a truthful answer?

Jonah guessed he could see why she wouldn't. She didn't even know them, and they knew too much about her. But why had she hunted up him and Chip anyhow? Had Chip even mentioned Jonah when he'd talked to Daniella on the phone?

"Um . . . did you come looking for us because your neighbor told you about us? Did she say we were on the middle-school welcoming committee, or something like that?" Jonah asked.

"*Are* you?" Daniella asked. She leaned in close. She was probably six or seven inches shorter than Jonah—physically, she shouldn't have seemed any more threatening than a kitten. But Jonah took a step back.

What am I supposed to say? Jonah wondered. *Should I admit we asked her neighbor nosy questions about her family? Should I tell her we know her original identity?*

"How did you find us?" Chip asked. He put his hand on Daniella's shoulder, maneuvering her to the side slightly, probably neutralizing any attack she might have been planning to launch against Jonah.

That's how you do it, Jonah told himself. *You ask a question instead of answering hers. All that stuff about "the best defense is a good offense" probably dates back to the medieval battle strategies Chip learned in the 1400s. It's not just one of those things coaches say.*

Daniella seemed to be blushing.

"You called me," she said. "So I had your cell number, and then, uh—"

"But I never even told you my name," Chip said. "And Verizon doesn't give out customers' info to total strangers."

Chip's voice stayed polite, and his face gave away nothing. At times like this, Jonah thought Chip really had missed out, not getting to stay in the 1400s and rule over his country for years and years and years. He could have been a good king.

Of course, if Chip had stayed in the 1400s, he would have ended up dead before he left his teens.

"Well, um . . . ," Daniella began. She lifted her chin defiantly. "For your information, you weren't the only one who contacted me."

What was that supposed to mean?

Jonah looked to Chip, because Chip seemed to be handling all of this better than Jonah was.

"Who else called you?" Chip asked in a low voice.

Daniella smirked ever so slightly.

"Wouldn't you like to know," she teased. "Let's just say there were evidently lots of people who couldn't wait for me to move to Ohio."

Did my friend JB contact you? Jonah wanted to ask. *Or— did Second? Did Gary and Hodge?*

Second and Gary and Hodge were Jonah's enemies. It was distressing that he could more easily imagine them getting to Daniella rather than anyone he trusted.

No, Second's gone off into another dimension, and he promised to leave original time alone, Jonah reassured himself. *And Gary and Hodge are still in time prison. Aren't they?*

Just a couple months ago, Jonah probably would have blurted out all the names, all his questions. But he had learned a little caution on his dangerous trips through time. It would be much better if they could get Daniella to tell them what she knew before Jonah or Chip revealed anything.

Chip raised one eyebrow—putting on an act again. Acting as if it didn't matter in the least if Daniella told them anything.

Jonah tried to imitate Chip's expression.

Daniella started to giggle.

"He said the two of you could be kind of funny," she snorted.

"'He'?" Jonah asked, trying to sound as if he didn't care that Daniella was laughing at him. And as if he'd caught her revealing some huge clue about her informant's identity, when really all she'd made clear was that it was a guy.

At least we've narrowed it down to half the world's population, Jonah thought. *We know Daniella wasn't secretly talking to, say, Katherine.*

Of course, he wouldn't have believed that, anyhow.

But thinking about Katherine made him wonder why Katherine hadn't shown up at the door—because of hearing Chip's voice, if nothing else. Chip and Katherine had kind of become boyfriend and girlfriend after the trip to the 1400s. But given that Katherine had ended up traveling with Jonah to three different centuries after that, Jonah guessed it wasn't exactly a normal middle-school relationship.

At least Katherine was doing better with Chip than Jonah was with Andrea, the girl he liked. Andrea had given him the "let's just be friends" talk after they'd both returned from the 1600s. Jonah hoped he might be able to change her mind someday, but so far that hadn't happened.

Don't think about Andrea right now. . . . Should I be worrying about what Mom and Katherine are finding online that would keep Katherine away from Chip?

Daniella had gone back to watching him and Chip very carefully. No—she had one of her own eyebrows raised, mocking them.

Jonah turned around and pulled the door open just a crack.

"Hey, Katherine?" he hollered into the house. "Want to come out here for a minute? There's someone you might want to meet."

Maybe Katherine could figure out how to deal with Daniella. Sometimes girls were better at understanding other girls.

A moment later Katherine pushed her way out the door. But—so did Mom. The last thing Jonah needed was Mom figuring out that something weird was going on.

"Hi," Daniella said, holding out her hand. "I'm Daniella McCarthy. My family just moved here today."

Jonah saw Katherine's eyes widen. As soon as Mom and Daniella were distracted shaking hands, Katherine mouthed silently to Jonah and Chip, *Is that who I think it is?*

Jonah winced and nodded. Then he looked quickly toward Mom to make sure she hadn't seen him wincing and nodding.

Mom actually looked a bit dazed herself.

"Wow," she was saying to Daniella. "Has anybody ever told you you look almost exactly like . . . ," She caught herself and shook her head quickly. Jonah wasn't sure if she was telling herself *That would be impossible* or *No kid wants to hear that she looks like some girl who's been dead for nearly a century*. But Mom put on a polite smile. "Sorry. I guess it's the power of suggestion. Retained images on the eyeball, or something like that. My daughter and I were just looking at some pictures online and it just made me think . . . um . . . have you met Katherine?" She kind of pushed Katherine forward. "Where did you say you moved here from?"

It had been a long time since Jonah had seen his mom act so flustered. It wasn't like she was actually going to figure out that this really was Anastasia Romanov standing before them, but still. She was making him nervous. How could he get Mom to go away without making her even more suspicious?

Now Daniella was shaking Katherine's hand and saying, "I'm from Michigan. Ann Arbor, Michigan." And the whole time she was watching everyone carefully, observing Mom's befuddled fumbling, and Katherine's eyes widening all over again at the mention of Michigan.

"And you say you just got here today?" Katherine asked, her voice too high-pitched and curious.

Mom began looking suspiciously at Katherine, too. Katherine dug her hand into her sweatshirt pocket.

"Kath—," Mom began.

Just then, the phone rang inside the house.

"Oh, excuse me. I'd better get that," Mom said.

She disappeared back into the house.

Now it was Daniella looking at Katherine with wide-eyed amazement.

"You use that trick too?" Daniella asked. "I thought my parents were the only ones who didn't have caller ID on their landline."

Jonah realized what had happened: Katherine had secretly called the home phone on her cell, just to get Mom to go away.

Katherine flipped a strand of her long blond hair over her shoulder and smiled angelically.

"It's only going to work for a minute," Jonah said. "She'll be back as soon as she picks up the phone and nobody's there."

Katherine kept smiling.

"But we won't be here when she comes back," she said. She opened the front door again and hollered inside, "Hey, Mom? Dad? Jonah and I are going down to Chip's for a little bit. Okay?"

She didn't wait for an answer.

"Smooth," Daniella said admiringly.

Devious, Jonah thought. *And—likely to get us in trouble, since, technically, we didn't get permission.*

But he stepped down from the porch with everyone else. The four of them walked through the yard and out to the sidewalk in an uncomfortable pack. Jonah wished he could pull Chip and Katherine aside and confer with them: *Should we just tell Daniella everything? Is it fair to keep her in the dark? How much should we worry about whoever else she's been talking to?* Of course there was no way to do this without Daniella noticing. But Jonah glanced around anyway, on the lookout for hiding spots between his house and Chip's.

That was how he first noticed the boy crouched behind the shrub in the next-door neighbor's yard.

Jonah elbowed Katherine.

"Do you think that's—," he began.

He wanted her to tell him the boy was just one of the neighborhood kids playing hide-and-seek or capture the flag. It was a little early in the school year for the high-school kids to be out playing senior tag, but who knew, maybe this was a particularly ambitious senior class.

Jonah didn't even get to finish his sentence.

Katherine was just starting to turn and look toward Jonah, when suddenly the boy sprang out from behind the shrub and lunged at them. Jonah saw only the boy's clothes: jeans and running shoes and a black sweatshirt, with the hood of the sweatshirt pulled forward to cover most of his face. And then the boy was grabbing all of them, pushing Jonah and Katherine together with Chip and Daniella, trapping them in his long arms.

"Now!" the boy cried.

Everything else around them disappeared.

FOUR

"You set us up!" Katherine screamed at Daniella.

"I did not!" Daniella screamed back. "I didn't know . . . Where are we? What's happening? Where are we going?"

Her voice held pure, stark terror, so Jonah was inclined to believe that she was telling the truth. Or that if she had set them up, she hadn't known where it would lead.

"Relax," Jonah said. "You're not in any danger. Well, not right at this moment. I know it's hard to believe, but we're traveling through time right now." He looked around at the familiar blank darkness of Outer Time. The only lights were far off in the distance, rushing toward them. "There's a lot that somebody should explain to you, but for now you don't have anything to worry about."

"How can you be so sure?" Daniella screeched. Jonah could barely see her, but he could tell that she was whipping her head from side to side in panic. If she wasn't careful, she might end up giving herself whiplash.

"Me and Katherine—well, and Chip, too—we've got a lot of experience traveling through time," Jonah said, trying for a soothing tone.

"Not like this," an unfamiliar voice growled near Jonah's ear. "Not in this direction."

Jonah turned his head to the side and made out the dim outline of a black hooded sweatshirt.

"You mean—" Katherine began.

"That's right, Katherine," the boy said mockingly. "This time we're going to the future."

Katherine gasped. For all Jonah knew, Chip and Daniella might have done the same thing, but Jonah blanked out of the conversation for a moment.

The future . . . ? Why . . . ?

Jonah wormed his right arm out of the boy's grasp and reached out to knock the other kid's hood back from his head. The boy's face shone pale in the dim light, his hair unnaturally dark.

"You!" Jonah snarled.

"You know who I am?" the boy taunted.

"Alexis Romanov!" Jonah accused, because he'd just figured that out. "And—"

Before Jonah could explain the other identity he knew

for the boy, the boy suddenly let go of Katherine and Chip and Daniella. They floated ever so slightly away. But the boy kept his hold on Jonah. He slid his hands up until he had them cupped around Jonah's neck.

"Don't call me that!" the boy screamed. "Anyway, it should be Alexei, but—I am not Alexis *or* Alexei Romanov! I refuse to be him!"

Chip and Katherine and Daniella struggled back toward Jonah and the boy. They began tugging on the boy's arms, pulling him back from Jonah.

"What is wrong with you?" Daniella asked the boy. "You never said anything about wanting to choke anyone to death! Or about traveling through time—"

"You were one of the kids with skulls on their sweatshirts, weren't you?" Katherine asked. "That day at the time cave—"

"And you were the one who helped Gary and Hodge!" Chip accused.

Jonah rubbed his hands against his neck, trying to rub away the soreness where the boy had grabbed him. He felt dizzy. Could he be suffering from oxygen deprivation just from the one second the boy had had his hands around Jonah's neck?

No, I've just got a lot to figure out, Jonah decided.

He thought back to the time cave, the day of the

adoption seminar at Clarksville Valley High School. It seemed centuries ago, even more distant in time than the 1400s. And really, in Jonah's life the adoption seminar *was* more remote and long ago than his trip to the 1400s or any other time period he could remember visiting. He had lived through the time-cave experience first.

The boy in the black sweatshirt had been there that day, part of a group of surly kids who'd been mean to Jonah and Katherine. Jonah hadn't seen the kid's resemblance to Alexei Romanov at the time, because he hadn't been looking at hundred-year-old pictures back then. But Jonah remembered this kid in particular because, at a moment in the time cave when the kids had taken control from all the conniving adults, this boy had secretly tipped the balance of power back to Jonah's enemies Gary and Hodge.

Didn't that make this kid Jonah's enemy too?

And Daniella—whose side is she on? Jonah wondered. *How does she know this kid? And—if he's working for Gary and Hodge again, does that mean they've escaped from time prison somehow? And sent him to do their dirty work? Does JB know about this?*

There were too many questions to deal with all at once. Maybe that was why Katherine and Chip had fallen silent too.

Not Daniella.

"Where's the information you promised me about my birth parents?" she demanded, staring at the boy in the black sweatshirt. "Or was that just a lie to get me to talk to these kids? Do you even—"

The boy flicked his gaze from Daniella to the others and back again.

"Later," he growled.

"Why should I trust you, anyway?" Daniella asked. Even floating through Outer Time she looked and sounded fierce. She put her hands on her hips. "I don't think you even told me your right name. You said you were Gavin Danes. Who's this Romanov person they're talking about?"

"I *am* Gavin Danes!" the boy shouted back at her. "I've got nothing to do with any Romanovs!"

"Gavin," Katherine said softly. "When Gary and Hodge offered to send you to the future, they were going to turn you back into a baby again, to be adopted by total strangers. So you wouldn't be Gavin Danes anymore. You'd be somebody else."

"That was the deal for *other* people," Gavin said wildly. "They offered me a special deal! In exchange for—"

He broke off, as if afraid to reveal too much.

Yeah, look around, Jonah thought. *Regardless of what side Daniella's on, you're still outnumbered.*

At the moment, anyway. Who knew what would

happen once they landed wherever they were going?

Jonah could see the lights beyond them, spinning closer and closer, brighter and brighter. What if Gary and Hodge had done something to make him and the other kids younger? When would it start? How much time did they have left?

"Are Gary and Hodge back?" Jonah asked quickly. "Did they break out of time prison? Did they give you your own Elucidator, so you could come and kidnap all of us?"

Elucidators were the devices time travelers used to move from one time period to another. But they were tricky things, able to take on the appearance of any common item from any century. They might look like a cell phone or a candleholder or a compass or a rock.

"Where is it?" Chip demanded. "Where's the Elucidator?"

He grabbed the other boy and began ransacking his clothes. He shoved his hands into Gavin's sweatshirt pockets, turned his jeans pockets inside out, even grabbed his shoes and felt around the laces.

Good idea, Jonah thought, and joined Chip in patting down Gavin.

"Elucidator, don't take us to the future!" Jonah screamed, just in case it was still on some voice-activated control. "Don't make us babies again! Take us back where we were! Where we're supposed to be!"

Jonah was hoping for some sense of instant reversal, of gliding backward. But it was impossible to tell what direction they were going. Because right at that moment they hit the point in the trip where Jonah always felt totally disoriented. Everything sped up. The lights ahead of them—or behind? Or just surrounding them?—whirled closer and closer.

"What's happening?" Daniella screeched. "What did you do?"

"I—" Jonah wanted to explain, but he was being flipped about so violently he couldn't force the words out. He knew he was still tumbling freely, but he felt pinned in place, his jaw forced open, his face distorted. He felt like he was being pulled apart and put back together, and every cell in his body hurt.

And then he landed.

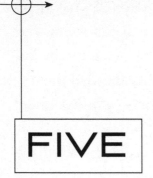

FIVE

"Where . . . ," Daniella whimpered. "Where are we?"

Jonah's vision swam in and out, unable to focus on anything.

Need to remember . . . something important . . . need to warn Daniella . . . , he thought vaguely.

He hated the symptoms of timesickness that always greeted him when he arrived in a new time period. It wasn't just that all his senses went on the fritz for the first few moments; his brain blinked out of service too.

Like now. There was something he should be telling Daniella, something he should be concerned about. But his brain couldn't come up with anything but *Shouldn't you worry about . . .*

"Shh," he heard Katherine whisper to Daniella. The sound seemed to come from a million miles away, but

Jonah was relieved to be able to hear it at all. And he was glad that Katherine had figured out she needed to warn Daniella.

"Don't make any noise until you're sure it's safe," Jonah tried to whisper too. But he hadn't regained enough control of his body yet. The words just came out as a long, drawn-out "unnhhh . . ."

And, anyhow, wasn't there something else he should be worrying about too? Something that he or Katherine or JB almost always tried to do to prepare for landing in a new time? What was it?

Jonah's brain seemed to be going *unnhhh* . . . as well.

Maybe it would help to try to see where they were? To figure out what they might be facing?

Jonah blinked hard, willing his eyes to work properly again. Fuzzy shapes moved around him. He remembered arriving on Henry Hudson's sailing ship in James Bay in the year 1611: the way they'd been surrounded by fog, and the way the only sound he could hear was the *thump-thump, thump-thump* of wet rope against wet wood.

This wasn't like that.

These fuzzy shapes around him seemed to be swaying in and out of sunlight—blocking the sun, unblocking it, blocking it again. Jonah could feel the pattern of shadow and glare sweeping across his face.

So those shapes . . . are they maybe tree branches? Or . . . some other kind of plants? Are we in a park or garden? Or just someone's yard?

Jonah felt like a genius for figuring out that much. Now if only he could think of the important thing he needed to remember . . .

"You!" someone suddenly screamed nearby. "You aren't supposed to be out here now!"

Jonah remembered what he'd forgotten before: invisibility. It was always wise to get the Elucidator to make you invisible before you arrived in a new time period. Otherwise you never knew what you might end up having to deal with.

But it was obviously too late to scream out, *Elucidator! Make us all invisible! Right now!* Especially if that "You're not supposed to be out here now!" was aimed at one of them.

But it sounds like the "you" being yelled at is someone the yeller recognizes, Jonah told himself. *Maybe . . . maybe we're all still safe? Maybe I'm just overhearing some other, unrelated conversation?*

Jonah turned his head slowly toward the sound of the yelling. His vision was improving. He could see thick green stalks around him now, and beyond that, Daniella lying sprawled in the middle of a pathway.

And what was that above her? Connected to the big yellow *M* on her blue Michigan sweatshirt?

No, not connected, Jonah thought, blinking again and again, trying to make sense of what he was seeing. *More like . . . pointing toward her? Pushed against her?*

His vision cleared. His brain unscrambled, and he decoded the sight before him.

Daniella was indeed lying on the path, her face twisted with terror.

Above her, a man in a khaki uniform bent menacingly over her body.

And between the two of them . . .

Between them, the man had a gun jammed against Daniella's chest.

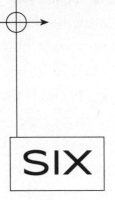

SIX

"What are you doing out here? Who gave you those bizarre costumes?" the man screamed at Daniella.

For a moment Jonah thought he was suffering from double vision as a side effect of the timesickness, because now he could see two uniformed men holding two guns against two kids' chests, and both chests were rising and falling in panicky breaths. Then he realized there really were two of everything: two men, two guns, and two kids—both Gavin and Daniella were pinned to the ground by soldiers holding guns.

But—just those two? Jonah wondered.

He turned his head silently, looking all around for Katherine and Chip. He saw no sign of them. Maybe, if they were lucky, they were hidden from everyone's sight.

And—what about me? he asked himself. He guessed that

the green stalks around him, whatever they were, had sheltered him from the uniformed men as well as the sunlight. But maybe that was just because the men hadn't looked his way yet.

He held his breath, not wanting to make the slightest sound to draw attention to himself.

"Answer me!" the man hovering over Daniella screamed in her face.

Was he a guard? A soldier? Jonah decided to think of the uniformed men as guards, because that seemed slightly less threatening.

"I—I'm sorry!" Daniella wailed. "I don't understand what you're saying! I don't know what you want!"

What language was the guard speaking?

Long ago, before one of their earliest trips through time, JB had made it possible for Jonah and Katherine to understand and speak any language they encountered in any foreign time. Jonah didn't fully understand how it worked, but he'd gotten so used to the help that he often didn't even bother paying attention to whether he and the people around him were speaking English or Serbian. (Which was a language he'd become very accustomed to on his last trip through time, to 1903.)

Obviously, Daniella had never gotten that language help—and neither had Gavin. He was also flailing about on the ground under the point of the gun, screaming, "Stop! Please! I don't understand!"

"Quit that foreign garble!" the guard above Gavin screamed. "Speak Russian!"

Okay, so I guess that's Russian, Jonah thought.

His body was hit with a wave of chills.

The guards are speaking Russian, and . . . those guns don't look like they're from the twenty-first century or the future, and . . . where in time would Russian guards have worn uniforms like that? They look old-fashioned but not centuries-and-centuries-ago old-fashioned. . . .

With a jolt, Jonah remembered what he'd tried to get the Elucidator to do when they were floating through time: *Take us back where we were! Where we're supposed to be!* Those instructions might have worked fine if they had all been like Katherine, bona fide twenty-first-century Americans. But they weren't. Even though Jonah still didn't know who or where he was supposed to be, he knew Chip was really supposed to be Edward V in the 1400s.

And Daniella and Gavin are really supposed to be Anastasia and Alexei Romanov from the early twentieth century, Jonah thought, horror breaking over him. *The Elucidator would know that too.*

Every Elucidator Jonah had ever used had had an annoying way of interpreting commands a little too literally. Jonah could see perfectly well how the Elucidator might have decided that since two of the kids in their group "belonged" in the twentieth century, that's where it would send the entire group.

Beyond the protective green stalks around Jonah, Gavin was begging the guards, "Please! Stop hurting me! I don't know what you're saying!" And Daniella was pleading, "English? Can't you speak English?"

"Russian!" the guard above Daniella roared. "Speak Russian *now*, or we will shoot you both!"

It would be my fault, Jonah thought. *It's all my fault we ended up here!*

He shoved himself off the ground. His legs were still trembling from the timesickness, but they were sturdy enough to bring him upright. Now he towered over all the plants around him.

"Stop!" he screamed in Russian. "Don't shoot!"

SEVEN

Instantly both guards whipped their guns away from Gavin and Daniella. Instead they pointed the guns directly at Jonah.

"Uh, hi?" Jonah said weakly. He was pretty sure this also came out in Russian, but it was hard to analyze something like that with guns pointed his way.

So what year would the Elucidator think Alexei and Anastasia belonged in? Was it 1918? How accurate were guns in 1918? Jonah wondered.

He decided they were probably much too accurate to risk trying to run away.

Not that he had anywhere to run to.

And not that he would be capable of running right now. He was doing well just to be able to stand up.

He swayed a little dizzily.

"Who are you? Where did you come from? How did you get in?" one of the guards barked at Jonah.

In? Jonah thought confusedly. Maybe he was wrong about being in some park or garden or yard? He looked around. Trees, grass, sky . . . he was definitely outdoors. But was that a wooden fence off to his right, encircling this yard and a fancy-looking building nearby? Was "inside the fence" what the guard meant?

"Well, uh, you see . . . ," Jonah began. "I was just . . ."

Just what? His brain stalled. How could he explain anything when he didn't know where he was or why the guards were so upset about him being there?

"He's bizarrely dressed too," the other guard pointed out. "Perhaps he brought them those clothes to help them escape."

The first guard took a step closer to Jonah. Jonah could see straight down the barrel of the gun.

"You were plotting an escape attempt?" the guard accused.

"N-no?" Jonah said. But his uncertainty came through in his voice. Even to his own ears, it sounded like he was lying.

The gun he was staring into inched even closer. How close would the guard have to be before he just decided to shoot without asking any more questions?

Suddenly, off to his left, Jonah saw Katherine pop up from behind a bush.

"Oh, there you are!" she cried.

She strolled toward Jonah, her motions as casual as if she walked in front of loaded guns all the time.

"Sorry," she said over her shoulder toward the two guards. "My brother's a bit simple. He doesn't understand."

Jonah understood perfectly well what happened next: Both guards now aimed their guns at Katherine.

"Don't shoot her!" he yelled.

Katherine laughed.

"See?" she said. "He just thinks we're all playing war."

The guns stayed trained on Katherine.

"What *are* you playing?" the first guard growled.

Katherine made a show of looking down at her sweatshirt and jeans.

"Duh," she said. "Dress-up."

The guns twitched a little. The guards seemed to be having trouble deciding if they wanted to aim at Katherine, Jonah, Daniella, or Gavin.

Okay, Katherine, Jonah thought. *At least you've managed to confuse them.*

But the guards still had horribly fierce expressions on their faces. They looked like, if they had their preference, they might just end up shooting all of them.

"No outsiders are allowed in here!" the first guard yelled.

"Relax," Katherine said. "My brother and I are from the

convent. We just brought in the day's shipment of food."

Where did Katherine come up with this stuff? Maybe she was just making it all up, but at least the guards kept listening to her. Neither of them was squeezing the trigger yet.

"And the nuns sent these dress-up clothes, too, for the, um, grand duchesses and the tsarevitch to use," Katherine continued. "We were just—"

Katherine must have said something wrong, because suddenly the closest guard swung his gun around and hit her with the butt of it. He must have hit hard—she immediately crumpled to the ground.

"They are no longer the grand duchesses and the tsarevitch!" the guard screamed at her. "They are nothing more than ordinary citizens! No better than anyone else!"

"Okay, okay—sorry!" Katherine protested, holding her hand up to head off any more blows. "I won't call them that again!"

Jonah realized that Daniella, still sprawled on the ground, had begun letting out frightened wails, and Gavin was crying, "What's going on? What's going on?"

"Just—keep calm," Jonah muttered. "Hold on."

But that was ridiculous advice, because he himself couldn't stay calm. Was there anything he could do to help Katherine? And—oh, yeah—where had Chip landed?

Was he in danger of being discovered any moment now too?

Before Jonah had a chance to decide anything, the first guard grabbed Katherine by the back of her sweat-shirt and pulled her to her feet. Then he reached out and grabbed Jonah by the arm.

"I'll take care of these two," the guard said.

"And I'll take the prisoners back to their rooms," the other guard agreed, pulling up Gavin and Daniella.

"No, stop!" Gavin cried. "Careful—I bruise easily!"

"Please! Somebody—help!" Daniella screamed.

She was looking right at Jonah. Jonah struggled against the guard's grip, but either the guard was extraordinarily strong or Jonah was still weak from the timesickness. There was no way for Jonah to break free.

"You'll be all right," Jonah said in English to Gavin and Daniella. "They're just taking you back to your rooms."

"What rooms?" Daniella demanded. "Where are we? Who are these people?"

But Jonah didn't have a chance to reply before the guard holding his arm yanked him away. And then Jonah had a more immediate question to worry about:

What was the guard going to do with Jonah and Katherine?

EIGHT

"If we were plotting to help the prisoners escape, why would we bring them weird clothes that make them more noticeable, not less?" Katherine argued, even as the guard dragged her and Jonah toward the imposing white building behind them.

The guard took his hand off Jonah's arm just long enough to hit Katherine in the head again.

"Shut up!" he commanded.

"I'm just trying to make you see that we deserve a fair trial if you're going to—" Katherine kept arguing.

"Stop talking!" Jonah yelled at her.

He felt the guard lifting his hand again, and this time Jonah reached out and tried to pull back on the guard's arm, so at least he wouldn't hit Katherine so hard. Jonah was rewarded for this: The guard slammed the palm of his hand against Jonah's head instead of Katherine's.

Can you get a concussion just from someone hitting your head? Jonah wondered.

The force of the blow was so hard that Jonah couldn't see or hear for a full minute. When his vision recovered, he saw that the guard had brought them to the top of a staircase leading down into a dim cellar. The guard gave them a shove.

"No, please . . . ," Jonah cried.

But it was useless. He and Katherine tumbled forward—forward and down. There must have been two dozen stairs before them. Jonah tried to grab on to the edge of the steps or some railing along the wall or something—anything! But the best he could do was just slow his fall. He kept plunging down and down and down . . .

He landed on top of Katherine.

She didn't move.

"Kath?" he whispered. "Katherine?"

No answer.

Jonah rolled to the side—painfully—and grabbed Katherine's shoulders.

"Katherine? Are you awake?" he asked, shaking her gently.

Still no answer.

He realized there was something else he should be

checking for. His hands shook as he moved one hand from her shoulder to the side of her neck.

Just find a pulse, he told himself. *Stay calm and just find her pulse.*

His fingertips felt so numb that he brought the other hand up to the other side of her neck. What if the pulse was there but he just couldn't feel it? He pressed down harder with both hands.

"Gah—now you're trying to strangle me?" Katherine moaned.

Jonah hugged his sister's shoulders. Then he scrambled back a little.

"I wasn't sure you were alive," he said, the relief making his voice tremble.

"I'm still not sure," Katherine groaned. "You're the Boy Scout—how do you tell if a bone's broken?"

"Does anything hurt?" Jonah asked.

"Does anything *not* hurt—that would be an easier question," she grumbled. She gingerly sat up and gasped. Even in the dim light, Jonah could tell that her face went pale. "My arm—"

"We can splint it in place with a sweatshirt until we get out of here," Jonah said. He quickly pulled his sweatshirt over his head and tied the sleeves together, then slid it around Katherine's shoulder.

"Better than nothing, I guess," Katherine said, letting her arm relax into the improvised sling. "But—how do you think we're going to get out of here?"

Jonah looked back toward the door at the top of the stairs. It was shut now and probably locked or guarded.

"Let's find some other way out," he said. "I don't think we should wait until the guards come back and get us."

He helped Katherine up, and the two of them inched forward, through an open set of double doors into another room. Jonah saw what seemed to be the only source of light: a single, naked lightbulb burning overhead. Its glow was so feeble that Jonah could barely make out the arch of the ceiling or the frame of another doorway and padlocked doors across from him. But there didn't seem to be much in the room worth looking at, anyway: It was just bare walls and a bare wooden floor. Jonah squinted, his eyes adjusting. One section of the wall, high overhead, might once have contained a window, but it was filled in now, completely covered. Jonah wished for some sort of furniture—a chair or a small table or something else he could stand on or use to slam through the locked doors or the filled-in window. But there was nothing.

Katherine made a gagging sound.

"That wallpaper!" she groaned.

Jonah squinted, making out stripes on the opposite wall.

"You want to criticize the decor at a time like this?" Jonah asked. "Sure, it's ugly, but who cares?"

Katherine clutched his arm with her free hand.

"No, Jonah—I've seen that wallpaper before! I recognize it! We're in the cellar!" she moaned.

Jonah wanted to make a joke to get her to sound less serious—something like, *Dub, Katherine, the guard just threw us down twenty-some steps. Of course we're in a cellar now!* The pre-time-travel Jonah would have said that. But now he just said in a calm voice, "What do you mean? What cellar?"

Katherine tightened her grip on his arm.

"Jonah, there were pictures of this room on the computer," she whispered. "Mom and I saw them after you went to get the door back home. This room . . . this is where the guards are going to kill the entire Romanov family."

NINE

Jonah felt like his sister had punched him in the gut. Hard. It took him a moment before he could trust himself to say, "But we know it hasn't happened yet. Because the guards weren't surprised to see Anastasia and Alexei—I mean, Daniella and Gavin—alive. So we've still got time to stop everything."

"How?" Katherine asked. "We don't have an Elucidator and we're trapped here and my arm's probably broken and, sure, as far as we know Chip's still safe up there and hasn't been caught, but *he* doesn't understand Russian and neither do Gavin and Daniella and—"

She broke off suddenly because the door at the top of the stairs creaked open.

"Your story was full of lies," the guard's voice shouted down at them. "The food delivery was hours ago, and of course nobody new was involved. The commander will be interrogating you soon."

Jonah and Katherine exchanged terrified glances.

"And it has been determined that you deserve no light," the guard added. He must have flipped a switch, because the naked lightbulb overhead suddenly blinked out. Then the guard slammed the door, plunging them into darkness.

For a moment Jonah and Katherine could do nothing but stand in shocked silence. Then Jonah heard Katherine taking ragged, gasping breaths, as if she was crying.

Jonah reached out to pat her shoulder in the dark.

"Hey," he said. "We'll figure something out. Or— maybe JB will rescue us."

"How would he even know we're missing?" Katherine challenged. "How could anyone find us? Even Gary and Hodge—even if they're the ones who gave Gavin the Elucidator—they wouldn't have expected him to bring us all *here*."

Somehow Jonah could hear more of the fear in her voice in the darkness.

"Yeah, but don't you think Gary and Hodge could track the Elucidator?" he asked.

"Maybe, but what if they can't?" Katherine countered. "Or they just don't bother? Or what if they're still in time prison and so they can't do anything, but they won't tell anyone else where we are because they don't want to get into more trouble?"

She was right. That did sound like something Gary and Hodge would do.

"It's all my fault we ended up in 1918," Jonah muttered, slumping over.

This was worse than the mess-up they'd had trying to return their friend Andrea to her past. Their enemy Second had sabotaged that trip and sent them to the wrong year. But at least JB had known it when they went missing. And he'd known to search for them.

Are Gary and Hodge out of time prison and searching for us right now? They'd want to look for us, too, wouldn't they? If only to make money, not because they'd actually care . . .

It was horrible that Jonah was now pinning his hopes on the possibility that Gary and Hodge had escaped from time prison. That he was now counting on two of his three worst enemies to save him.

You've got to think of something else, he told himself.

"Katherine, let's at least try feeling along the wall and the floor," he told his sister. "Maybe we'll find a key to these padlocked doors, or, I don't know, a release for a secret passageway out of here. . . ."

Jonah was grateful that Katherine didn't say, *That's ridiculous* or *You think this is a fairy tale or something? You think we're all going to end up happily ever after?*

Instead she muttered, "Okay."

In the absolute darkness Jonah couldn't see where Katherine went. But he heard her pained, awkward footsteps moving toward the wall, and her fingers trailing against the despised wallpaper. Then the brushing sound stopped.

"Jonah, I'll feel around on the floor, but I can't touch that wall," Katherine said. "I keep seeing it in my mind the way it looked in the pictures on the computer. There are going to be huge chunks of this wall missing, where the bullets hit. . . ."

Thanks a lot for putting that image in my head, Jonah thought. He lifted his own hand from the wall, then resolutely put it back, moving methodically side to side.

"Katherine, it doesn't have to happen that way," Jonah said. "It hasn't happened yet, so there's still time—"

"Jonah, you didn't read what I read. The whole family's going to be herded into this room, and then a bunch of guards are just going to start shooting them—nobody could survive that," Katherine said. "It's, like, hopeless."

Jonah hated the way just that one word made him feel like giving up. Especially with all this unrelenting darkness around him.

"You had, what, five or ten minutes more than I did looking at that stuff on the computer?" he challenged Katherine. "That doesn't make you an expert! Maybe there's something you don't know about, something that's going to make this all work out."

Jonah expected her to say something like, *Yeah, well, you don't know anything, so how's that going to help?*

Instead she cleared her throat. It almost sounded like she was embarrassed.

"I guess you're right," she said. "It's like, I shouldn't have said that thing about being from the convent. I didn't know it would get us in worse trouble. I just thought I was so smart because I read online about food deliveries from a nearby convent. . . ."

Katherine's admitting that I'm right and she was wrong? Jonah marveled. *Does this mean miracles really are possible?*

Jonah didn't get even a split second to gloat over this turn of events, because the door at the top of the stairs creaked open again.

"The commander will see you now," the guard announced.

The man was so high above them at the top of the stairs that Jonah could see only boots silhouetted in the doorway. None of that light trickled down to him and Katherine, so Jonah couldn't see how his sister reacted.

"Should we hide down here and make them come and find us?" Jonah whispered.

"There's nowhere to hide," Katherine said hopelessly. "I think that would just make them madder."

Jonah figured Katherine was right, but it was so hard to force himself to trudge toward the stairs.

You can't make Katherine be the first one to face that guard, Jonah told himself.

He shuffled forward. Though he couldn't see her yet, he heard Katherine beside him moving in the same direction. Even when they reached the bottom of the stairs, they still stood in pitch darkness. Jonah cupped his hand over his sister's ear.

"If there's just that one guard who came for us, let's try to overpower him," Jonah whispered. "We'll knock him out and run away."

Jonah felt, rather than saw, Katherine nodding. His heart pounded. It was a crazy plan, but just having something to hope for gave him the courage to start climbing.

First step. Second. Third . . .

Unlike Katherine, Jonah didn't think he'd broken anything falling down the stairs. But climbing back up them made his muscles scream out about how sore his whole body was. He was hardly in peak fighting condition, and Katherine probably did have a broken arm. And no matter how fierce she was, she wouldn't come up any higher on the guard than his elbow, and—

Eighth. Ninth. Tenth.

Jonah kept climbing.

We are going to fight that guard if he's alone, Jonah told himself. *We're going to fight him and we're going to win.*

Jonah was on the fifteenth step and peering grimly up to the top when suddenly a hand grabbed him from behind. Jonah teetered, almost falling over backward.

"Do you want me to land on you again and break your other arm?" he muttered, whirling around to confront Katherine. "Focus!"

It annoyed him that he couldn't see his sister well enough to glare at her. Even this close to the doorway, the pool of darkness behind him seemed so complete he could barely make out Katherine's shape. It was like she was just an outline.

"I mean it," he scolded her. "We've got to be ready to fight!"

"Look at me!" Katherine whispered back. "Look at yourself!"

Jonah looked.

Outline . . . Katherine's just an outline. . . . And me? Hey, look at that, there's a little bit of that light coming in from the door and it's . . . it's flowing right through me. I'm see-through! Someone made us invisible!

Jonah made a triumphant fist pump in the air. Behind him he could see Katherine grinning up at him. He knew he was the only one who could see it—when time travelers became invisible, people native to that time could see nothing of them. But other time travelers could make out their invisible colleagues as translucent figures, as if they were made of glass.

Now that he wasn't expecting Katherine to appear as anything more than a see-through outline, he could easily read the expression on her face.

"This is so great!" he hissed at her.

But even as he watched, her grin vanished.

"No," she whispered, her eyes wide with horror. "No . . ."

Jonah whirled back to face the guard, to see what she was seeing.

"If you do not come right away to see the commander, we will come to you," the guard at the top of the stairs shouted down at them.

What seemed like dozens of feet started trampling down the stairs, as guard after guard raced toward Jonah and Katherine. Each of them held a gun aloft—a gun with a gleaming knife strapped alongside its barrel.

Invisible or not, if Jonah and Katherine didn't move immediately, they were both going to be bludgeoned or stabbed to death.

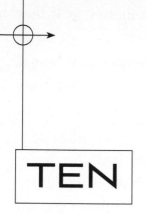

TEN

"Run!" Jonah screamed, and he didn't even care if the guards behind him heard.

He began scrambling back down the stairs, taking them two at a time. Katherine was too close, and he stepped on the back of her shoe, pulling it half off. She bent down to fix it, and he hollered, "No time for that!" She wasn't reacting fast enough, so he dashed around her, reaching out to pull her along with him at the last minute.

He got a firm grip on her sweatshirt, and after a moment Katherine clued in and matched his stride. But the staircase was really too narrow for both of them to run practically side by side. With each leap Jonah took it was touch and go whether he would stay upright or fall, knocking both of them down to smash against that hard floor again. How many bones would they break this time?

Please don't let us fall, he thought, which was maybe a

prayer and maybe just instructions to himself.

Jonah kept running. But the guards were running faster.

The frontmost guard was only three steps behind Jonah. Now two. Now—

Now Jonah leaped for the floor and whirled off to the side, pulling Katherine with him. He flattened his back against the wall, and he saw that she did the same.

"We just have to wait until the guards are past and then we can escape up those stairs," Katherine whispered.

Jonah nodded and put his finger over his lips. It was a great plan, except that the guards were spreading through the cellar, waving those gun-knife contraptions all around.

Bayonets. His mind came up with the proper name for them. *They're bayonets.*

Jonah was annoyed that his mind wasn't doing something more useful, like figuring out how to avoid all the bayonets being waved near him. Someone had turned the one solitary lightbulb back on, but its light was so weak that none of the guards seemed to trust it. They were blindly thrusting their bayonets into all the dark corners, toward every wall.

"Back to the stairs?" Katherine whispered in his ear.

Jonah nodded.

"As soon as the last guard's out of the way," he whispered back.

But the whispering had distracted him—Katherine

had to pull him to the side to avoid one of the bayonets.

He tiptoed back toward the stairs, dodging bayonets right and left.

This is even worse than dodging torches, he thought, remembering the hazards he and Katherine had faced on one of their earlier trips through time.

The guards had stopped streaming down the stairs, but two of them stood on the bottom step, guarding the way out. Jonah ducked under the one guard's elbow in an attempt to slip past him. But just then the guard leaned back, cutting off the space between the wall and the stairs. Jonah could still fit in that space, but he was at such an awkward angle he wasn't going to be able to launch himself upward. He was bound to fall over backward, crashing into the guard. He wobbled. He wanted to scream for Katherine to help him, to give him a push, but that would just attract the guards' attention. His mouth opened anyway, involuntarily.

"H—," he began.

But before he could get out the rest of the word "help," a hand appeared out of nowhere and pulled him up.

ELEVEN

The hand was translucent. It was attached to an equally translucent wrist and arm, covered in what seemed to be the translucent sleeve of a sweatshirt.

"Chip!" Jonah started to scream. At the last minute he turned it into a mere mouthing of the word. But he grinned at his friend to let him know how completely relieved he was to see him. Or, well, to see *through* him.

For Chip had also evidently been granted time-traveler invisibility.

Get Katherine and let's get out of here, Chip mouthed back at him, pointing past Jonah as if he didn't trust Jonah to get the message otherwise.

Jonah nodded and turned to pull Katherine through the gap between the guard and the wall. Now all three kids stood on the stairs above the guards. The guard nearest them turned around and gazed suspiciously in their direction. Had he sensed Jonah and Katherine brushing past him? Had he heard Jonah's barely breathed "H—"?

It didn't matter. He couldn't see them, so he didn't start climbing toward them or waving a bayonet up at them.

Chip tugged on Jonah's arm and made a *C'mon* motion with his hand, gesturing toward the open door above them.

Before someone decides to shut the door, he mouthed.

Jonah nodded, and all three kids began tiptoeing up the stairs.

Jonah almost felt like giggling.

Ha, ha, ha, he wanted to shout down at all the guards scanning the cellar so thoroughly. *Thrust your bayonets anywhere you want—you're not going to catch us! You'd have to be able to see us to find us!*

They escaped into the sunshine outside the cellar door. They looked around and, by silent agreement, tiptoed on out toward the wooden fence at the far side of the garden, where no one would hear them.

"Great timing!" Jonah congratulated Chip as they both flopped to the ground. Katherine eased down beside them.

"I was terrified that I might be too late," Chip said. Even though he used modern words, he still sounded vaguely medieval. His face grew serious as he turned toward Katherine. "Oh, no—*was* I too late?"

Jonah looked at his sister. She still had his sweatshirt tied as an impromptu sling around her arm and neck. One of the bayonets must have connected, because the sleeve of her own sweatshirt had a gaping hole in it now, right over her bicep. But no blood stained the sweatshirt, so maybe the bayonet had only gone through the cloth, not her arm.

Also, her frown looked more annoyed than pained at the moment.

"Chip, I am not some damsel in distress you had to rescue!" she protested. "Jonah and I were doing fine by ourselves!"

"No, we weren't," Jonah said. "Katherine may not be grateful, but I'm glad you rescued us!"

Chip looked confused. He reached out and gingerly touched Katherine's elbow.

"But your arm—"

"Is fine," Katherine said quickly. She tugged off the improvised sling made from Jonah's sweatshirt and handed it back to her brother. "It just hurt a little at first, and you know, Jonah's a Boy Scout, so he had to prove he was prepared and all. . . . It's nothing."

What was this—Katherine actually downplaying an injury, rather than acting like breaking a fingernail might kill her?

Jonah would never figure out his sister. Unless . . . was this all for Chip's sake?

Chip was still peering anxiously at Katherine.

"I was so afraid you would think I was a coward when I didn't jump up and fight when the guards started dragging you away," he said. He shoved back his hair—an odd sight, given that it looked crystalline and see-through now, as if each of his normally blond curls had been turned into glass. "I didn't want you thinking me a coward, but—"

"But what you did was perfect," Jonah interrupted.

He thought he kind of saw what Chip and Katherine's problem was, but the last thing Jonah wanted was to become their relationship coach.

"Look," he told them. "We don't have time right now for the two of you to work out your 'I want to be your knight in shining armor' / 'Oh, no, you don't; I can take care of myself; this isn't 1483 anymore' issues."

He imitated them in such ridiculous, mincing voices that Chip and Katherine both protested: "We don't sound like that!" Then, realizing that they'd each said the exact same thing, they stopped and gazed into each other's eyes.

Oh, brother, Jonah thought. *Young love. Ick.*

Jonah grabbed each of them by the arm to get them to look at him. Katherine winced slightly.

Oops, Jonah thought. *Guess I grabbed the sore one.*

But she didn't say anything, so he ignored it.

"Help me out here," he said. "Let's just figure out what we need to do next—as a team. Don't you think we should rescue Gavin and Daniella? Chip, if you were able to make us all invisible, that must mean you got Gavin's Elucidator away from him after all. So why don't you pull that out, and—"

"Jonah, I don't have Gavin's Elucidator," Chip said, shaking his head so hard it made his curly hair bounce up and down.

"Then how'd we all end up invisible?" Katherine asked.

Chip tilted his head to one side.

"I thought I made it happen, but now that you question me, mayhap I could be wrong," he began slowly.

This was something else that made Chip's medieval moments particularly maddening: He could take forever thinking through things.

"Just tell us what happened," Katherine said.

"With twenty-first-century words," Jonah added. "And speed."

Chip got the hint.

"I was behind a bush when we landed here, so I was pretty sure that none of the guards would see me," he began. "I couldn't understand what anyone was shouting about, but I thought if Gavin had an Elucidator with him and it was voice activated, then maybe I could just whisper, 'Make me invisible,' and it would happen."

Jonah wished he'd thought of that himself, before he'd jumped up and started yelling at the guards.

"But that didn't work," Chip said.

See? Jonah told himself. *It doesn't actually matter that I was stupid.*

"So then what did you do?" Katherine asked.

"Well, by then that one guard was dragging you two away, and I knew I had to do something drastic," Chip said. "I crawled over as close as I could get to Gavin."

"Wasn't the other guard taking him and Daniella away too?" Katherine asked.

"No, for some reason he was acting like he needed the first guard to come back and help him," Chip said. "Like he didn't think Gavin could walk or something."

"That's weird," Jonah said.

"No, it's not," Katherine said. "Alexei Romanov had to use wheelchairs a lot. Because of the hemophilia."

"What's that mean, anyway?" Jonah asked.

"Mom told me—it's something about blood not clotting right," Katherine said. "So I guess if he got even, like, a little cut, he could bleed to death."

Jonah didn't quite get how that was connected to wheelchairs—were Alexei's parents afraid that if he stood up and walked on his own, he might fall down and get hurt? Jonah wasn't going to ask, because he wanted Chip to move along with his story.

But Chip was just staring at Katherine.

"Wait a minute," Chip said. "You're saying Gavin, who's really Alexei Romanov, who's that kid who was lying on the ground over there a few moments ago—he's got this disease where he could bleed to death from a little cut?"

"Yeah," Katherine said.

It didn't seem possible, given that Chip was already translucent, but he suddenly looked paler. Maybe it was because of the horrified expression on his face.

"Oh, no," Chip said. "Oh, no. Do you think it's a problem that I just slam-tackled him?"

TWELVE

"You did *what?*" Katherine asked.

"That was what I had to try next!" Chip said defensively. "I didn't know the kid had medical problems!"

"But why tackle him?" Jonah asked, still puzzled. "I mean, I know Gavin kind of attacked us first, but—".

"That's not why I did it," Chip protested. "It was just logical."

Jonah waited to hear how this could possibly be logical.

"See, I figured out that if Gavin had an Elucidator, it couldn't be voice-activated from a distance," Chip explained. "Since it worked for you before, when you were holding on to Gavin, I thought that you must have been touching the Elucidator without knowing it. The second guard was coming back, and I knew I didn't have much time, so I just jumped out from the bushes and slammed

Gavin flat on the ground so I was right on top of him and the Elucidator, and then I screamed, 'Make me invisible!'"

In a weird way this did kind of make sense. The Elucidator might have been set up to take voice commands only from someone who was touching it.

"Okay, um, and that worked?" Katherine asked skeptically.

"Yeah!" Chip said. "I've been invisible ever since. And then I real quick said, 'Make Jonah and Katherine invisible too.' And then the second guard was back and I had to roll out of the way. And since neither of the guards was looking in my direction when I tackled Gavin, and they couldn't understand English anyway, I was totally safe."

Jonah couldn't decide if Chip had been crazy brave, or just crazy.

"Why didn't you say, 'Make all five of us invisible'?" Katherine asked. "To protect Gavin and Daniella, too?"

"I thought that might mess up time, since this really is the time they belong in," Chip said. He winced. "I didn't know tackling Gavin could kill him."

There was an eerie silence in the garden around them. Jonah hoped it was just his imagination getting to him.

"You didn't . . . see any blood, did you?" Katherine asked slowly.

"No, but I don't think Gavin was conscious when the guard picked him up," Chip said. "I thought maybe he was just pretending to pass out so they wouldn't keep yelling at him, but . . . what if he really was dying?"

Having those words hang in the air was even worse than the silence.

"Stop saying things like that," Jonah said firmly. "Gavin is not going to die from you tackling him. If we mess up history, that's not going to be the way we do it. Because we are right now going to go find Gavin and Daniella and the Elucidator. And then we're going to make the Elucidator take us back to the twenty-first century, where Gavin can get good medical care. And everything is going to be *fine*."

He hoped he sounded more confident than he felt. He tried to remember the first-aid training he'd gotten in Boy Scouts. Surely if someone was going to bleed to death just from being tackled, it would take a long time, wouldn't it? Definitely longer than the fifteen or twenty minutes that might have passed since Chip had tackled Gavin?

Jonah stood up and was relieved to see that Chip and Katherine did the same.

"Did you see where the guards took Daniella and Gavin?" Jonah asked.

"Into that house," Chip said, pointing toward the

building above the cellar where Jonah and Katherine had been trapped. "I'll show you which door they used."

Even as he trailed after Chip, Jonah squinted up at the arches and frills of the imposing house—or was it a mansion? Or a palace?

Probably not a palace, he decided. If the tsar of Russia had been in charge of a sixth of the entire planet, his palace would probably have been much more impressive than this. Jonah knew kids back home who lived in houses about this big and fancy. But now that Jonah was looking more closely, he started noticing some strange details: Under the soaring arches at the top of the house, all the windows seemed to be whited out from the inside, like in an abandoned factory. And why was there such a crude wooden fence around the whole property? Why were there guardhouses inside the fence—like maybe the danger was inside the fence too?

Chip crouched beside a tree.

"That one," he said, pointing to a door beside the one Jonah and Katherine had gone through to get to the cellar.

Guards still swarmed in and out the cellar door, undoubtedly continuing to search for Jonah and Katherine. Jonah was more concerned about the two who stood at attention by the second door.

"We'll have to wait until those guards leave, right?"

Chip asked anxiously. "So we don't mess up history by making them think a door just opened and shut on its own?"

"No," Jonah decided. "Not if there's a chance that Gavin's in that house bleeding to death."

"Forget history," Katherine agreed.

Chip recoiled slightly and gaped at the two of them. If Jonah hadn't been so worried about Gavin—and their chances of finding the Elucidator and getting home safely—he would have laughed at Chip's horrified expression. Chip had been on only the first time-travel trip with Jonah and Katherine. Jonah felt like he'd gotten about a million more years' worth of experience since then.

It made a difference.

"Come on," Jonah said, taking the lead once more.

He tiptoed right up to the door and twisted the knob. He did try to do it silently, but he let the door swing all the way open so Chip and Katherine could come in with him.

Behind him, he heard the guards let out a string of curses.

"Why didn't you make sure that door was latched?" one yelled at the other.

"Me? You were the last one through!" the second yelled

back. "Have you been drinking already? If the commander finds out, with what he has planned for tonight—"

What's planned for tonight? Jonah wondered. *Never mind— we'll be gone by then.*

The guards didn't recover from their arguing to shut the door until all three kids were safely inside the house. Jonah turned to Chip and held up his hands in a *See? Wasn't that easy?* gesture. But as both guards struggled to pull the door closed again, Jonah saw that they separated completely from what seemed to be ghostly doubles of themselves.

Ugh, Jonah thought. *Tracers.*

During his trips through time, Jonah had developed a love-hate relationship with tracers, the eerie, ghostly representations of how time would have gone if time travelers hadn't intervened. On one of the trips, to 1611, time had gotten so messed up that all the tracers had disappeared. Jonah had missed them then, and he had been delighted when they'd reappeared. But most of the time when tracers showed up, they just seemed like nagging reminders: *You're messing up time. What if you mess it up so badly that it can never be fixed?*

Jonah told himself that two guards arguing and having to shut a door was nothing in the grand scheme of things.

"Think we should go upstairs?" Katherine whispered,

pointing to a nearby staircase. "The guards were taking Gavin and Daniella to their 'rooms.' Bedrooms, maybe? Don't you think bedrooms would be on the second floor?"

This made sense to Jonah. All three kids began tiptoeing up the stairs. Some of the wooden steps creaked, but Jonah didn't care. He couldn't see anyone around close enough to hear it.

"Ahh!" Katherine practically shrieked as they approached a landing. "What's that?"

It looked like a bear rearing up on its hind legs above them.

It is *a bear,* Jonah told himself. *But it's stuffed. No worries.*

He saw that Chip had flung himself protectively in front of Katherine, as if to make sure that if anyone was going to be mauled, it would be him, not her.

"Stop acting like fools," Jonah hissed. "It's dead."

But the word "dead" seemed to echo in the dim stairwell. And when Jonah stepped up on the landing beside the bear, he saw that there were also stuffed bear cubs hunkered beside the mother bear.

"Creepy," Katherine whispered. "Who wants to keep dead animals inside the house?"

"Maybe it was just an ordinary thing in this time period," Chip said defensively. His own time period, the 1400s, had so many weird and creepy things that he was maybe a little sensitive about anyone criticizing anyone else's time.

"What's creepy is all the people looking down here now, because Katherine screamed," Jonah muttered. He looked up at three more guards clustered beside the railing above him, along with a plump woman who seemed to be wearing a maid's costume.

Jonah glanced at his own hands and then at Chip and Katherine just to make sure that they were all still invisible—they were.

Move along, people, Jonah thought, as if he could mentally direct the onlookers. *Nothing to see here. You just imagined you heard a noise. That's all.*

But they all kept staring, seeming unusually rattled when they probably couldn't have even heard Katherine that well.

And anyhow, why are there so many guards around? Jonah wondered.

Was it just because they were still looking for him and Katherine, escapees from the cellar? Or was there something else going on?

Jonah pushed those questions to the back of his mind and concentrated on tiptoeing the rest of the way up the stairs. He moved past the tracer of the maid, who looked just as much on edge as the version of the woman who'd heard Katherine shriek. Next, he and

Chip and Katherine entered a large dining room, which held an ornate wooden table beneath a chandelier.

See? This may not be a palace, but it is a mansion, he thought. *The kind of place royalty might visit on an ordinary day.*

But just then two more uniformed guards walked by.

Mansion or prison? Jonah asked himself. *Which is it?*

He glanced into the living room, where a man sat writing in a notebook and four women sat hunched over books or needlepoint. Three sleeping dogs lay at the man's feet. An abandoned chess game lay by his elbow.

"That's the tsar, the tsarina, and Anastasia and Alexei's three older sisters," Katherine whispered in Jonah's ear. "Olga, Tatiana, and Maria."

Jonah would not have figured this out for himself. The tsar looked like a gardener, maybe, in workman's clothes. The oldest woman—the tsarina, Jonah guessed—sat in a wheelchair, her face gaunt and anguished. The three girls who had looked so beautiful in all the pictures were now distressingly thin, as if they were nearly starving. Instead of lacy white dresses and pearls, they wore plain black dresses. It wasn't just that they looked older now, grown-ups instead of children. They also looked pinched and desperate and despairing.

It looked like they had given up.

Then one of the sisters glanced up and caught the eye

of one of the guards. She winked at him, then went back to staring down at her sewing.

Okay, maybe that one hasn't given up, Jonah thought. *Still . . .*

"There are beds back in this other room," Chip whispered in his ear. "Let's try this direction."

Jonah took Katherine's arm and pulled her away from the living room. They followed Chip back through the dining room and then into a room containing four army-style cots.

Where the guards sleep? Jonah wondered.

But there were dresses and skirts hanging along the wall, rather than uniforms.

So is this maybe Anastasia's room? And her sisters'? Jonah wondered.

He was back to thinking of this house as a prison again.

Another door led out of the room, and Katherine was already pushing through it.

"It's them!" she whispered back excitedly to Jonah and Chip.

Both boys immediately crowded into the doorway beside her.

Now Jonah could see Daniella—or was it Anastasia?—sitting beside a bed, reading out loud from a book on her lap.

"'If it is our duty to honor our responsibilities, then . . .'

Oh, Alexei, I think you're asleep now anyway, so I'll just skip the boring parts," she was saying. She hit the spine of the book against her leg for emphasis. This made the skirt of her plain black dress flare out.

Dimly Jonah realized that he wouldn't be seeing or hearing her—the real Anastasia, in her real early-twentieth-century clothes, just like her sisters'—unless Daniella had indeed been brought to this room and joined with the original version of herself. He knew how it worked: Daniella's sweatshirt and jeans and the rest of her twenty-first-century appearance would have been swallowed up completely when she became Anastasia again. If Daniella were somewhere else, he would see only a ghostly, pale tracer.

And, oh yeah, she was speaking Russian now. That was proof.

"You're right—there's Daniella/Anastasia. But what about Gavin?" Jonah whispered back to Katherine as he tiptoed past her and Chip, on into the room.

And then Jonah gasped.

Gavin/Alexei lay on the bed in an old-fashioned nightshirt, his covers kicked off to reveal a swollen, bandaged knee. One of his elbows hung at a painfully awkward angle, also swollen and engorged. Even in sleep his face was twisted in pain.

If the rest of his family had looked defeated, Alexei looked completely destroyed.

Behind Jonah, Chip murmured in dismay, "Is that what I did to him? Is he going to die?"

THIRTEEN

Chip had spoken too loudly—Anastasia/Daniella glanced up at the sound of his voice.

No, Jonah corrected his own perceptions. *It's just Daniella looking this way. Not Anastasia. See the tracer?*

The original version of Anastasia continued peering down at the book, her lips still moving in what seemed to be the even cadence of reading aloud. But Jonah couldn't hear anything she was saying now, and her lips glowed with tracer light. Daniella's face pulled away from the tracer's ever so slightly, bafflement spreading across her expression.

"We've got to pull her out," Katherine muttered. "What do you bet she's confused beyond belief?"

Without waiting for an answer, Katherine went over and tugged on Anastasia/Daniella's shoulders. A moment later Daniella lay sprawled on the floor, once again looking like a twenty-first-century girl in her jeans and Michigan sweatshirt. The Anastasia tracer, meanwhile, continued silently reading, sedate in her simple dress.

"What in the world is going on?" Daniella thundered.

Jonah dived toward her and clapped his hand over her mouth.

"Shh!" he hissed. "We'll tell you, but you have got to keep your voice down. You don't want those guards coming back, do you?"

Daniella's eyes got big, and she quickly shook her head no.

"I'll be quiet," she whispered from underneath Jonah's hand.

Jonah moved his hand back.

"And I thought moving to Ohio was a nightmare," Daniella groaned, in a much softer voice. "Wait—that's what all of this is, right? A nightmare? You're all practically invisible, and everything's freaky, so of course this is just one big bizarre dream, and all I've got to do is wake up and then—"

Her voice was inching upward again. But all Jonah had to do was scowl at her and she stopped.

"Daniella, I'm sorry there's not more time to explain, but all of this is real," Katherine whispered, leaning down to pat the other girl's shoulder sympathetically.

"Of course it is," Daniella said sarcastically. "Oh, I get it . . . if this isn't a dream, then I've gone totally nuts. I told my parents I wouldn't be able to stand the move, and I was right. I'm crazy now."

"You're not crazy," Chip said softly.

"How else do you explain the fact that it's like I'm two people at once now?" Daniella challenged. "Everything Anastasia would know, everything she would do, I—" She turned around, getting her first glimpse of her own tracer. "Eek! Th—that's me! It's her! It's me!"

Her voice was a little too loud again, but Jonah thought it would only make things worse if he grabbed her once more.

"Let's just get out of here and then tell her everything," Jonah said. He moved toward Gavin/Alexei. The boy moaned in his sleep.

"But do you think Gavin is safe to travel?" Chip asked.

Jonah hesitated. He turned to Daniella.

"What do you know . . . I mean, what does Anastasia know about her brother's hemophilia?" he asked.

Daniella clenched her jaw.

"We don't talk to outsiders about Alexei's problems," she snapped. "We don't even acknowledge they exist . . . Gah! It's like she's inside my brain, thinking for me!"

She began hitting the palm of her hand against her

forehead, as if that could knock the Anastasia identity out of her mind.

"Daniella, it's okay to tell us," Katherine suggested.

Daniella kept her mouth shut.

"Can you at least tell us how long Gavin's looked this bad?" Chip asked. "Gavin, not Alexei?"

Daniella squinted at Chip, confusion playing across her face.

"Only since . . . he and Alexei became the same person?" she said hesitantly. "Like Anastasia and I kind of became the same person? The guards put us in this room, and then, I don't know, it was like I *had* to walk into that ghost-person Anastasia, and I did, and suddenly it was like I *was* Anastasia, and I knew everything she knew, even Russian. And Gavin just kind of fell onto the bed and became Alexei, and . . . that doesn't make any sense at all, does it?"

"Yes, it does," Chip said comfortingly. "I know exactly what you're talking about. Because I went through exactly the same thing more than four hundred years ago."

Daniella just gave him another confused look.

"Do you think maybe that means it's Alexei who's in such terrible shape, and it'd be safe to pull Gavin out?" Katherine asked.

"I think we have to try it," Jonah muttered.

He put his hands on Alexei/Gavin's shoulders and

gently pulled upward. The boy on the bed winced and moaned. But after a moment Gavin was sitting upright, apart from the Alexei tracer. He once again had the black sweatshirt on; his hair was slightly longer than Alexei's, with a dyed dark-purple streak on one side. He blinked and looked around.

"Have a heart," he begged. "Pull me the rest of the way out."

Jonah tugged, and Gavin rolled over onto the floor, landing on top of Jonah. Gavin instantly pushed away. He stood up and massaged first his elbow, then his knees.

"I didn't know it could feel that bad," he muttered. "What that kid puts up with on a daily basis . . ."

He shook his head in seeming disbelief.

His joints were all normal-size now, no longer swollen, no longer bandaged.

"You're not bleeding?" Chip asked. "You're not going to bleed to death because I tackled you?"

"You thought I was going to bleed to death?" Gavin sneered. "Do you *see* any blood on me?"

He held his elbows out at odd angles, as if inviting Chip and the others to look. Then a flash of fear spread across his face.

"Is it happening?" Daniella asked. "Are you getting that feeling?"

Gavin whirled toward Daniella.

"You know about that?" he asked.

"I think . . . I think we really are brother and sister," Daniella said. "It's like I've known you practically my whole life. *This* whole life. . . . Er, *are* you okay?"

Gavin didn't sneer at her.

"It's not that bad," he said.

"What are you two talking about?" Katherine asked.

"If you must know, I think Chip might have started an internal bleed in my hip when he tackled me," Gavin snarled. "I'm really good at sensing these things." He punched Chip's arm. "Thanks a lot!"

So, it's a problem for Chip to tackle Gavin but okay for Gavin to punch Chip? Jonah thought.

He decided against saying that out loud.

"Oh, well, bleeding inside isn't as bad, is it?" Katherine asked. "If the blood doesn't actually leave the body . . ."

"Idiot, internal bleeds can cause even worse problems, if you don't get treatment," Gavin said, sounding even surlier. "So, yeah, I could die from your stupid friend over there tackling me!"

Jonah stepped up between Gavin and Chip.

"Stop arguing," he said. "Let's just get out of here. So you won't die."

He was about to ask Gavin to just hand him the

Elucidator, but then he remembered that Gavin might still want to go to the future. So Jonah went with Chip's strategy: He slammed into Gavin, matching his arms and legs against Gavin's, and called out: "Take all five of us back to the twenty-first century! To the time where Katherine belongs!"

Katherine and Chip must have had the same thought, because they also rushed toward Gavin.

Chip cried, "Take us all back where we were when Gavin grabbed us to begin with!"

And Katherine called out simply, "Take us home."

Out of the three of them, one of them had to be touching the spot where Gavin had hidden the Elucidator, somewhere in his clothes.

But absolutely nothing happened. The world around them stayed firmly, stubbornly 1918.

FOURTEEN

Angrily, Gavin pushed Jonah and the others away.

"You think I didn't try that?" he snarled. "You think I didn't try to escape the minute I figured out where we are? Especially when I found out the date?"

"The date?" Daniella repeated, glancing back toward her tracer, who was still calmly reading. "What's wrong with July 16, 1918?"

Gavin looked at her, and for the first time his expression softened.

"Nothing," he said, almost sounding kind for once. "Don't worry about it. Nothing happens today."

Daniella kept staring back at him. Jonah couldn't tell what was passing between them without a single other word being spoken. He lost patience with trying to guess.

"Well, we know the Elucidator worked before, when

it brought us here and made Chip and Katherine and me invisible," Jonah said, trying to sound calm and reasonable. "Can you at least let us see the Elucidator? Katherine and I have used Elucidators a lot—maybe we can get it to work again."

"Fine," Gavin said, snarly again.

He reached inside his sweatshirt, maybe into a pocket of his T-shirt underneath. He pulled out . . .

A metal toy soldier.

"What the . . . ," Gavin muttered. He patted his sweat-shirt, all along his chest. "Is this a joke? I had the Elucidator right *there*. It looked like a cell phone. Did one of you just steal it?"

"Alexei loves his toy soldiers," Daniella murmured, as if trying to explain her brother to everyone. "He always car-ries a handful in his pockets—and bits of paper and chalk and string, anything for his little games. . . . Did you just carry that off from when you stopped being Alexei?"

"It doesn't work that way!" Gavin snapped at her. "Does it?"

He was appealing to Jonah and Katherine and Chip for the answer.

"No," Jonah assured him. "I bet that really is still the Elucidator. It's just, the Elucidator changes shape to fit in with the time period. So it won't look out of place."

"It is really freaky," Katherine said soothingly. "Our Elucidator looked like a compass in 1903."

"And a rock in 1483," Chip said, making a face.

"But how would you program it like this?" Gavin asked frantically, poking at the metal base of the soldier with one hand, the painted-on cap with the other. His efforts did nothing but chip off a tiny fleck of paint from the cap, exposing the bare metal underneath.

"Let me try," Jonah said, taking the toy soldier from Gavin. He was a little surprised that Gavin let him. Jonah squeezed his hand around the Elucidator and demanded: "Take all of us back to the twenty-first century!"

Nothing happened.

"Make me invisible!" Jonah tried again.

"You already *are* invisible," Katherine reminded him.

"Oh, right," Jonah said, feeling foolish. He already felt silly enough, talking to a little toy soldier. "Make Gavin invisible!"

He looked up just in time to see Gavin blink out of sight: The black sweatshirt, the purple streak in his hair, the surly expression on his face—all of it went see-through, all at once.

"It works!" Katherine cheered.

"Wh—what—?" Daniella stammered. "Are you *sure* this isn't all a dream?"

"Make Gavin visible again," Jonah commanded.

In a flash the other boy was back to normal. Daniella looked like she might faint, but Jonah decided this wasn't the time to worry about that.

"Let me talk to JB!" Jonah said into the Elucidator. "JB, are you there?"

No answer.

"JB? JB?" Jonah called.

Nothing. Jonah might as well have been trying to talk into an ordinary toy soldier, one that was nothing but solid metal all the way through.

"Let me try," Katherine said.

She took the soldier from Jonah's hand and started trying out all sorts of commands: "Call JB!" "Call anyone you can reach!" "Tell us how to get home!" Jonah could tell by her disappointed snort after each command that none of it was working. Chip and Daniella joined her in bending over the toy, throwing out more commands, some ridiculous, some down-to-earth.

"Bring me a Snickers bar!" (This was from Daniella.) "Show how much battery life you have left!" (From Chip.) "Wave at me and blink your eyes!" (Daniella again.)

As far as Jonah could tell, the Elucidator wasn't doing any of it. He turned his attention back to Gavin.

"Where did you get that Elucidator anyway?" he asked.

"What's it to you?" Gavin retorted.

"I just thought that might help explain—"

Gavin grabbed the front of Jonah's shirt.

"I don't have to explain anything to you!" he sneered. "Anything! Got it?"

"Not even how to save your life if you've got internal bleeding that could kill you?" Jonah asked.

Gavin's surly expression slipped for only an instant.

"I can handle my own bleeds," he said. "Back home, sometimes I don't even bother telling my parents for hours. And I'm fine! It's just so annoying to deal with."

"But you can get good treatment in the twenty-first century, right?" Daniella interrupted quietly, looking up from the Elucidator. "Here, remember, it's just ice and bed rest and—"

"I'm fine!" Gavin protested.

Jonah could hear Chip and Katherine's requests to the Elucidator getting more and more desperate.

"Well, if you can't do any of that stuff, can you at least tell us what you *can* do for us?" Katherine asked, sounding totally exasperated.

Out of the corner of his eye, Jonah saw a sudden glow of digital light near the toy-soldier Elucidator. He immediately crowded in beside Chip, staring at it.

Above the soldier's head, red computer-style letters

had appeared, as if on an invisible screen. They spelled out a single word: YES.

Then that word vanished, replaced by a short list:

I CAN:
- TAKE PEOPLE TO 1918
- GRANT INVISIBILITY
- UNDO INVISIBILITY COMMANDS
- LIST MY LIMITED FUNCTIONS

"That's all?" Katherine moaned.

YES glowed again over the soldier's head.

"But why? Why not anything else?" Chip asked.

Evidently, answering that question was outside this Elucidator's "limited functions," because the glow instantly disappeared and the Elucidator looked like an ordinary toy soldier again.

"This is like . . . like those cell phones people buy for little kids, where they're only set up to call Mommy and Daddy, and nobody else," Katherine complained. "It's useless!"

Gavin stared at her.

"You think this Elucidator was designed that way?" he asked.

"Well, yeah," Katherine said, with a defeated shrug.

"Or programmed that way, or something. Have you gotten this Elucidator to do anything else for you?"

Jonah waited to see what surly comeback Gavin would give Katherine. But Gavin just kept peering at her. He was squinting now, clearly puzzled.

"Yes, I did," Gavin muttered. "But that was before . . ."

A change came over his face, disbelief and confusion slipping away into fury.

"Oh, no," Gavin said. "Oh, no. Gary and Hodge tricked me!"

FIFTEEN

"I knew it!" Jonah exclaimed. "Gary and Hodge gave you this Elucidator, didn't they?"

"Who are Gary and Hodge?" Daniella asked.

Gavin sank back onto the bed, where his own tracer still lay in pained sleep. His hand slid over top of his tracer's hand, and he winced, as if the pain could flow from the tracer's body into his.

He jerked his hand back.

"I might as well tell everything," he muttered. He switched his gaze to Daniella. "Gary and Hodge rescued us. You and me, we were Alexei and Anastasia, and we were trapped here with our family, and they came and took us away. They wanted to take us to another time period, where we'd be safe and I wouldn't be sick. And then—"

"He means Gary and Hodge *kidnapped* you," Katherine

interrupted. "They took you away from where you belonged, and they were reckless and could have ruined history—"

"We're supposed to die, aren't we?" Daniella asked

She spoke so calmly that everyone stopped and stared at her.

After a moment Gavin said, "You know that's what Mama and Papa believe?"

Jonah could tell he was talking about their 1918 parents, the Romanovs, not anyone from the twenty-first century.

Daniella nodded.

"I know everyone thinks I'm just the little jokester, and I can't be serious for a minute, but—I've seen the kind of letters Mama writes," she said. "She believes this is our fate. 'Life here is nothing—eternity is everything, and what we are doing is preparing our souls for the kingdom of heaven.' She expects the guards to kill us. Soon. Papa hides it better, but he thinks that too. I think . . . I think they want us all to die together. They believe that would be better than going into exile in some other country."

Jonah realized he'd been foolish all this time, trying to think of this house as anything other than a prison. The Russian Revolution must have already happened; the tsar was no longer in charge.

And his entire family was being held prisoner.

"*We're* not supposed to die," Gavin told Daniella. "You and me. I saw it online. Alexei and Anastasia aren't killed and buried with the rest of their family. They're missing. So, see," he said, turning to Jonah, "doesn't it seem like, maybe, what Gary and Hodge did was actually right? Like this is how history is really supposed to go?"

"When did you see that online?" Katherine demanded. "Jonah and I were just looking today—I mean, today back home—and it said *none* of the Romanovs survived!"

Gavin gaped at her.

"What?" he said. "No—I just looked it up yesterday—yesterday when I was in the twenty-first century—"

"So what changed from one day to the next?" Chip asked.

"Did Gary and Hodge find a way out of time prison and mess everything up?" Jonah asked.

Gavin actually began to moan.

"What's wrong?" Daniella demanded.

"It was me!" Gavin wailed. "It's all my fault! I made it so we all have to die!"

And with that he plunged back onto the bed, rejoining his anguished tracer.

SIXTEEN

Jonah, Chip, and Katherine all moved together to pull Gavin back out.

"Churlish knave, you cannot just give up like that," Chip said, and Jonah hardly minded the medieval language, because Chip was trying so hard to separate Gavin from his tracer.

"At least tell us what you did before you hide behind Alexei!" Katherine insisted, tugging on Gavin's shoulders.

Jonah had the feeling that Gavin was fighting them, trying as hard as he could to stay Alexei.

"Look, we've been in plenty of impossible situations before, and we've found a way out," Jonah told him. "Sure, we don't have much of an Elucidator. Sure, we don't have any way to contact anyone. Sure, your family's in danger here." Jonah was depressing himself, listing all these obstacles. "But—we'll find a way out! I know we will!"

Jonah's hands kept slipping from Gavin/Alexei's arms.

Daniella perched on the edge of the bed, watching them intently. She looked completely baffled about what she might do to help.

"Even if you don't care anymore about trying to save yourself, don't you want to save your sister?" Jonah asked.

And suddenly Jonah could feel Gavin slipping away from his tracer, coming back. The dyed purple streak in his hair reappeared, then the black sweatshirt, then the unswollen joints.

"Save his *sisters*. Plural," Daniella corrected Jonah. "And his parents. How could Gavin or I try to save ourselves without helping the rest of our family escape too? I'm not going anywhere without the others!"

You're nuts! Jonah wanted to shout at her. Didn't she understand how difficult it was going to be just to save her and Gavin? Especially when they didn't even have a decent Elucidator? And now Daniella wanted to add five more people to the rescue mission—including a woman in a wheelchair? That was like asking to make their failure that much more devastating.

And what would it do to time if we rescued the former tsar of Russia? Jonah wondered.

Since the very beginning of his time-travel trips, Jonah had had trouble caring as much as his friend JB did about preserving time. Jonah cared a lot more about saving people's lives. Even though JB, as a time agent, was sworn to protect time, he had mostly come around to that viewpoint too. But Jonah had also seen that there were limits to how much time could be changed—and he'd seen the consequences of pushing those limits.

But how could he tell Gavin and Daniella that, when they were gazing at each other so hopefully?

Jonah sighed.

"Can you just give us some background here, before we figure out any plans?" he asked. "How did Gary and Hodge trick you? I'm guessing they broke out of time prison, gave you that dumbed-down Elucidator, and—"

"Oh, no," Gavin said, shaking his head emphatically. "I'm the one who broke them out of prison. I took control of things!" He sounded so proud of himself, but then his expression turned sheepish. "And—I guess I was the one who programmed that Elucidator to be worthless."

He took the toy soldier from Katherine's hand and flipped it across the room, where it crashed into an entire army's worth of similar-looking toy soldiers massed on the floor.

Chip went over to pick it up.

"Let's not be hasty," he said. "Mayhap this could still be useful, even despite its limitations."

Jonah expected Gavin to make fun of the medievalisms

creeping back into Chip's speech, but Gavin just sat on the edge of the bed, glowering down at his knees.

Chip carefully tucked the toy-soldier Elucidator into his jeans pocket.

"Gavin, could you please just explain everything from the very beginning?" Katherine asked. "I'm confused, and I bet Daniella has no idea what we're talking about."

Daniella rolled her eyes.

"I told my parents everything would be strange for me if we moved to Ohio," she said. "Little did I know . . ."

Then she giggled, and Katherine actually giggled with her. Chip gave a snort-laugh. Jonah guessed that, if they weren't in such a dangerous, confusing situation, Daniella would probably be one of those kids who kept everyone else laughing constantly.

Under normal circumstances, she probably wouldn't have had any trouble at all moving to a new town and a new school.

But none of this was normal.

"Okay," Gavin began. "Remember back at the time cave?"

"What time cave?" Daniella asked. "And what's a time cave, anyway?"

Katherine began giving Daniella a long explanation of everything that had happened after Gary and Hodge kidnapped her: the time crash, the thirty-six babies on the plane, the adoptions, the return of Gary and Hodge and JB to fight over all of them once again, after they were all thirteen.

"Wow, sounds like I missed a really great time!" Daniella joked. But she looked a little dazed—Jonah wasn't sure how much she'd actually absorbed.

"So anyhow," Gavin said, "in the time cave, all of us kids managed to overpower the adults."

Jonah opened his mouth to object—*he* was the one who'd managed to overpower the adults, no thanks to Gavin or any of Gavin's friends. Of course, Jonah had had some behind-the-scenes help from the one adult they'd known they could trust, a woman named Angela.

Katherine kicked Jonah while no one else was looking. Then she glared and shook her head, and Jonah could tell that she was trying to say, *Don't interrupt or he might stop talking. Just let him finish his story!*

"So we all split up the adults and kind of, like, interrogated them," Gavin continued. "I was in charge of talking to this one rescuer, Gary. Gary told me I couldn't trust JB, and he said that if I set him free, he would take me to the future, where I was supposed to go in the first place."

"You wanted that?" Katherine exploded. Clearly she'd forgotten about not interrupting. "You wanted Gary and

Hodge to make you into a baby again, so you'd forget all your friends and your family and your whole life?"

"Yeah, my adopted family, who hate me," Gavin said. "And my sucky life . . . who cares about all that? Anyhow, Gary said he'd make me a special deal. *I* wouldn't have to go back to being a baby again. Just the other kids."

Now it was Chip who interrupted.

"You'd do something like that to other kids?" he asked. "Kids you don't even know?"

Gavin wouldn't meet Chip's eye.

"Gary said they'd cured hemophilia in the future. Cured—one hundred percent!" he said. "So kids with hemophilia are no different than anyone else. They can play football just like anyone else, instead of having their moms say they can only do swimming, like mine always does. They don't have to have injections every third day, just to be 'normal.' They never get bleeds in spite of the injections. They *are* normal!"

Jonah noticed that Daniella was peering at Gavin with the saddest expression on her face. He didn't want another distraction.

"So you set Gary free, that day in the time cave," Jonah said, trying to sum up. "But he didn't stay free. JB sent him and Hodge to time prison right after that. So what's this story have to do with anything?"

Gavin smirked.

"Gary was really smart," he said. "He knew everything was risky and he might not beat JB that day. So before I even set Gary free that first time, he gave me this code, just in case he got caught again. He said if he and Hodge ended up in time prison, I should lay low for a while, then find an Elucidator somewhere and type in the code. And then, he said, I'd get everything I wanted."

"Yeah, how's that working out for you?" Katherine said sarcastically.

Gavin flushed.

"Look, *now* I know that Gary tricked me!" he protested. "Now I know he was lying when he said, 'This will get me out of prison and set you up *fine!*' But I believed it then. I thought he and Hodge were going to meet me in the future and treat me like a prince!"

He is treating you like a prince, Jonah thought. *A prince whose father's been forced out of power and is about to be killed.*

"Okay, let's back up," Jonah said. "Where did you find the Elucidator? It's not like they're just lying around for anyone to take, back home."

Gavin's face turned even redder.

"I kind of, um, borrowed it," he said. "Okay—I stole it! Remember that woman, Angela, who was in the time cave with us? I kind of spied on her afterward, because as far as I could tell, she was the only adult who stayed in the twenty-first century. And I saw this other time traveler, Hadley Correo, give her an Elucidator."

Jonah exchanged glances with Katherine and Chip. He wasn't sure how much of Gavin's story he could trust, but this part checked out. The time travelers from the future had given Angela an Elucidator so she could protect Jonah and Katherine.

Yeah, that was a great idea, Jonah thought.

This was the second time that that particular Elucidator had sent them into danger.

"So, I get why *you* would want to go to the future," Daniella said, peering intently at Gavin. "But why'd you grab the rest of us? What did we ever do to you?"

"Look, if we'd really ended up in the future, like I thought, you would have loved it too," Gavin said. "Remember how you've always hated being short? I bet in the future kids can arrange to grow to whatever height they want!"

Daniella narrowed her eyes at him.

"*I* don't hate being short," she said. "That's just how Anastasia feels. And anyhow, you grabbed us before you knew anything about her or me!"

Gavin grimaced.

"I know," he said softly. "Before I joined with my tracer and started thinking like Alexei, I . . . I didn't really care how you would feel about changing to a different time. I was just doing what Gary told me to do. I'm sorry." He cleared his throat. "Anyhow, Gary said I'd have an Elucidator and I could go back home anytime I wanted, if I didn't like the future. I guess I thought that would work for you, too."

And you believed that? Jonah wanted to taunt him. *How stupid are you?*

He bit his tongue, because he didn't think he could say anything else to Gavin without sounding really mean.

Daniella was squinting hard at Gavin.

"I don't get it," she said. "Did Gary and Hodge want us here in 1918 or in the future? Why is 1918 the only choice on the Elucidator if they promised you the future?"

She's right, Jonah thought. Was it maybe that Gary and Hodge had wanted them back in 1918 from the very start? Did that mean that it wasn't Jonah's fault that they'd landed here?

But why would Gary and Hodge want Gavin and Daniella back in the time period where they were in danger of dying? Wasn't their whole business based on taking famous kids from the past and making a lot of money adopting them out to families in the future?

"And—," Daniella said, as if she had lots of other questions she wanted to ask. But then she froze at the sound of footsteps coming from the next room.

"What should we do now?" she whispered.

Gavin didn't even ask. He just threw himself back together with the tracer Alexei.

"Oh, I see," Daniella muttered.

She leaped off the edge of the bed. She must have been aiming to land directly on the chair—squarely in her own tracer's lap. But she landed crooked, and the chair slipped out from under her. She hit the floor with a thud.

Quickly Jonah and Chip yanked her back up by the arms. Katherine slid the chair back into place and Daniella slipped into position just as the door opened.

It was the sister Jonah had seen wink at the guard. Jonah glanced back and forth between Daniella/Anastasia and her sister—how much had the sister seen? Had she been watching as twenty-first-century Daniella disappeared and turned into twentieth-century Anastasia?

The sister's blue eyes, so similar to Anastasia's, were wide and alarmed. But as soon as the sister spoke, Jonah understood that she had already been upset before she opened the door.

"When the guards found you in the garden . . . ," she began, her voice trembling. "Were you trying to escape? Without me?"

SEVENTEEN

"Oh, Maria," Anastasia murmured.

Jonah whipped his head back and forth, trying to watch both Anastasia and her sister—Maria? There had been a slight glow of tracer light around Maria's mouth when she spoke, which meant that in original time she had walked into this room at just this moment, but those words weren't the same as whatever she had originally said.

But Anastasia—she didn't have any tracer lights, so I guess she would have said, "Oh, Maria," even without time-travel changes, Jonah thought.

But what did the changes mean? Jonah was already pretty sure that in original time no guards had caught Anastasia and Alexei out in the garden. If time was supposed to go that way, Daniella and Gavin would have found their tracers outside.

So why had everyone landed in the garden when they came back to 1918?

Jonah didn't know. Poor Daniella/Anastasia knew even less about time travel than he did—what would she come up with to say to her sister?

For a moment, Anastasia just sat there with a dazed look on her face. Then she swallowed hard.

"Of course we weren't trying to escape without you," she whispered. She blinked back tears, as if the accusation hurt. "I wouldn't do that to my favorite sister! I wouldn't even do that to Olga!"

Jonah guessed that that was her least favorite sister. But he was too busy watching for tracer lights to think deeply about it. He had seen the glow of tracer light around Anastasia's mouth when she was talking about escaping— just a quick moment of her saying something different from original time. But then the light was gone when she talked about her sisters.

"So what were you doing out in that garden?" Maria challenged.

Tracer lights—check, Jonah thought. *So—not what she would have said originally.*

But how was Daniella/Anastasia going to answer *this*?

She didn't even hesitate.

"Oh, Maria, don't you ever feel like you're going to

explode if we have to stay cooped up in this house a minute longer? We've been here forever!" Anastasia complained.

"Seventy-eight days," Maria agreed. "This is our seventy-eighth day. But we did go outside to the garden for our morning walk, and then again after lunch. And they let us have mass on Sunday, and we talked to those peasant women who came in to clean yesterday—"

"And that's enough for you?" Anastasia asked. "We came back in from the afternoon walk today, and I was looking at the whitewashed windows, and I felt like I couldn't stand it another minute. I thought I would scream or go crazy or, I don't know, do something awful! And then I saw that, for once, there weren't any guards by the stairs, and so . . . I just had to have fresh air again!"

Strangely, the tracer light didn't show up until Anastasia's last sentence.

"But taking Alexei with you . . . ," Maria whispered. "How did you even get him down the stairs? How did you expect to bring him back up?"

This was all tracer light—all a departure from what she would have said originally.

"You carry Alexei up and down the stairs all the time," Anastasia said accusingly.

"I'm six inches taller than you," Maria said, and Jonah realized this was true. The two girls looked a lot alike, but they were built very differently: Anastasia was short and stubby, while Maria towered over her. And Maria looked much more muscular. Jonah thought that if she were a twenty-first-century kid, she'd probably be some big athlete—a shot-putter, maybe.

"You know I'm as strong as an ox," Maria continued. "But you—you could have dropped Alexei and hurt him."

"I wouldn't do that!" Anastasia insisted.

"Anyway, what were you thinking, refusing to speak Russian to the guards?" Maria asked. "Why did you want to make them mad?"

"It was just a joke," Anastasia said, sounding like a sulky little girl. Jonah was impressed with her acting skills. Because of course that hadn't been the reason she'd refused to speak Russian. Until Daniella had joined with the Anastasia tracer for the first time, she hadn't *known* Russian.

Maria came over and crouched down on the floor, right beside Anastasia's chair. Chip had to move out of the way so she didn't run into him. But all three of the invisible kids—Jonah, Chip, and Katherine—were leaning in close so they could be sure to hear everything Maria said.

"You know we've got to make sure the guards like us," Maria whispered.

The tracer lights disappeared completely with that

sentence. Maria would have said those words no matter what.

"I know," Anastasia whispered back. "I understand."

"*Do* you?" Maria asked. "Do you know how important this is?"

Anastasia nodded, her expression entirely serious.

"That's why I've been flirting with the guards so much," Maria went on. "Some of them . . . well, I'm pretty sure they wouldn't kill us if the commander gave that order. Igor is our friend, and Filipp, and probably Dmitri, too. And a few others. About the rest, though, I bet a lot of them wouldn't ever fall for my flirting. But you—everybody loves you. You're like the kid sister all of them want to protect. It's just not, well, you know, romantic."

"Thanks a lot," Anastasia muttered.

Maria reached out and ruffled her sister's hair in a way that kept her comment from being an insult.

"I'm not joking," Maria said. "You may be the only one who can save our family. You tell funny stories, and you stick out your tongue behind the commander's back, and *all* the guards love that. And . . . it changes things."

"Sticking out my tongue is supposed to keep us alive?" Anastasia asked. "That's all we've got to fall back on?"

"What else is there?" Maria asked bleakly.

Anastasia was silent for a moment. She glanced over at

Alexei, as if checking to make sure that he was still asleep.

"I think Mama wants to die," she said. "Wants to be a martyr, wants to fulfill God's will . . ."

Maria grabbed Anastasia's hand.

"Shush," she hissed, almost angrily. "How can she be so sure God wants us to die?"

"If that's what happens—isn't it meant to be?" Anastasia asked.

"And if we stop it, doesn't that mean that *that's* what God wants?" Maria asked. "How can we know ahead of time?"

Jonah's head spun. These were exactly the kind of questions he'd agonized over concerning fate and destiny, especially after his last trip through time. And Maria didn't even know about time travel.

He realized that he'd gotten so engrossed in the conversation that he'd stopped watching for tracer light. But had he missed seeing any? It seemed that ever since Maria had come to sit with Anastasia, the conversation had been just like it would have been in original time.

Suddenly Daniella separated from her tracer ever so slightly, just enough to peer up at Jonah and Chip and Katherine clustered around her.

"Maria, maybe there are others who could help us," she said, her lips just barely separating from the tracer

Anastasia's. "Not like before, when we got our hopes up and nothing happened. I'm talking about people the guards won't see. Like . . . like angels."

Jonah frowned and shook his head at Anastasia. It wasn't as if Maria was going to suddenly realize, *Oh, yeah, there are invisible time travelers from the twenty-first century in this very room with us, and they're going to intervene and help us all.* But it seemed dangerous to let her know anything before they had a firm plan.

"You mean, guardian angels?" Maria asked. "Believe me, I've prayed—"

She broke off, because just then the sound of a loud argument came from outside the room.

"I can't, I won't—you can't make us do that!" a man's voice screamed.

"Is that . . . Igor?" Maria asked.

She and Anastasia exchanged glances. Then, as if by silent agreement, both of them jumped up and fled the room.

EIGHTEEN

Of course Jonah, Chip, and Katherine followed the two girls.

All five of them—Anastasia and Maria in the lead, with the other three invisibly trailing a few steps behind—dashed through the bedroom with the camp beds and the dresses hanging on the wall, and then through the dining room with its solid wooden table and fancy chandelier. Then they got to the room where Olga and Tatiana and their parents were sitting. Anastasia and Maria slowed to a faked leisurely stroll.

The tsarina fixed them both with a severe look.

"Girls," she scolded, "proper young ladies should never involve themselves with the squabbles of servants."

"The guards are not our servants," Maria muttered under her breath, undoubtedly too softly for her mother to hear. "They're our jailers."

"And our lives could depend on knowing what they're saying," Anastasia muttered, just as softly.

The tsar said nothing. He just sat there gazing sadly at his daughters. He had lit a cigarette since the last time Jonah had passed through this room, and the smoke wafted around him. It was like a screen between the two youngest Romanov girls and the older members of their family.

Jonah leaned forward and whispered in Anastasia/ Daniella's ear: "I'll go see what the screaming is all about. Don't get in trouble over this if Anastasia wouldn't have done that originally."

Daniella separated from the Anastasia tracer just enough to move her head up and down once, quickly.

"Yes, Mama," Anastasia said, the picture of obedience. "I understand, Mama."

Jonah brushed past her into the only section of the second floor he hadn't seen before. It was like crossing a barrier from the family's quarters to an area that belonged completely to the guards. Within five steps he was peering into a filthy office where half a dozen guards lounged about. For the first time Jonah noticed that some of the guards actually had grenades attached to their belts; an array of guns lay across the top of a piano.

What if I grabbed one of those guns? Jonah wondered. *Could I do it without anyone noticing? Could I use it to protect the Romanovs?*

Would he have any clue how to use a gun from 1918?

Jonah left the guns alone. He looked around for the source of the screaming he'd heard before. This didn't take any great powers of deduction: Two guards had a third guard in a headlock, and the third guard was still sputtering, "I won't! You can't make me!"

"Igor, you're drunk," a man in a more impressive-looking uniform said disgustedly, as he stood regarding the guard. "What did you do, drink up all your wages this afternoon?"

"Not drunk!" Igor protested. "Didn't drink up my pay! Just—not evil like the rest of you! I swear I could never—"

One of the men who had him in the headlock clapped his hand over Igor's mouth. Now all Igor could do was squirm and moan.

"Get him out of here," the official-looking man commanded. "Tell his friend Filipp he's suspended from his evening shift too."

Igor, Filipp—those are two of the guards Maria said the Romanovs could trust not to kill them, Jonah thought with a chill.

As the other guards dragged Igor toward the stairs, Jonah raced back into the living room. Now Anastasia and Maria were sitting with their sisters, hunched over sewing projects of their own.

"Igor and Filipp aren't going to be working tonight," Jonah whispered in Anastasia's ear. He tried to make this news sound like it was no big deal, but Anastasia gasped out loud.

Everyone else in the room looked up at her, the movements creating a glow of tracer light around each person's head. It was startling in the dim room, in the haze of smoke.

"Oops," Anastasia said with a giggle, quickly covering her mistake. "Stabbed myself with the needle. Silly me."

"Don't get blood on that blouse," her mother scolded.

"Oh, I'm not bleeding," Anastasia said, holding up a clear, unpricked finger. "I promise."

Jonah had to admire her skill at lying. But he saw that the sleeve of a dark blue sweatshirt—Daniella's Michigan sweatshirt—appeared briefly around her wrist when she deviated from what Anastasia would have done in original time.

No one else seemed to notice, though, and the roomful of Romanovs settled back into their silent reading and sewing. All the tracer lights blinked out quickly, returning the room to its smoky gloom.

Jonah didn't know how any of them could bear to just sit there.

"Chip, Katherine, and I are going to scout around, see what else is going on," he whispered in Daniella/Anastasia's ear. "You just keep acting like Anastasia."

Daniella nodded, the motion so nearly imperceptible that Jonah barely saw any tracer light.

Jonah grabbed Chip and Katherine each by an arm and tugged them away from the Romanovs, into the deserted dining room. In a whisper he quickly explained what he'd seen and heard in the guard office.

"We've got to find out how much time we have," he told the others. "And what other allies we might have. Those guards we went past, coming into the house—they said something about what the commander had planned for tonight. But we don't know what it is, and—"

"Jonah, yes we do!" Katherine hissed. "Remember? Daniella said the date today was July 16, 1918. And remember what we saw on the computer back home? About how the entire Romanov family was executed in the early morning hours of July 17, 1918? Don't you think that's what the guards were talking about?"

Jonah had forgotten about seeing that date on the computer. It hadn't meant that much to him before he'd been in 1918, before he'd met any of the Romanovs. But now he staggered back against the wall.

Hopeless, he thought. *This is just hopeless.*

Even if "early morning hours" meant as late as five or six a.m., that could be less than twelve hours away.

"But remember, when Gavin looked online the day before you did, it said Alexei and Anastasia escaped,"

Chip said. "So isn't it possible that we could do something so that the next time anyone looks at a computer in the twenty-first century, it says that none of the Romanovs were executed? Because that's what really happens?"

Jonah couldn't tell if Chip was saying that because he really believed it, or if he was just trying to make everyone feel better. Either way, Jonah decided to go along with it.

"Absolutely," Jonah said. "Everything is still in flux."

He tried not to think about the look on Daniella's face when she'd said to Gavin, so calmly, "We're supposed to die, aren't we?" He tried not to think about how fate had seemed to take over on their last trip through time, to the extent that everything about their friend JB's life had come to seem preordained.

As if nothing they might plan to do could possibly matter.

"So," Jonah said, a little too brightly, totally faking it. "Where do you think we should start searching for information? Back with the guards or in Alexei's room? Don't you think there still might be some information Gavin isn't telling us?"

"Maybe we should split up," Chip said. "We don't want Gavin to feel like we're ganging up on him. Who do you think he'd trust the most?"

"Um, none of us?" Katherine said, rolling her eyes.

Jonah sighed.

"I'll go talk to him," he said. "You two see if you can find out anything else by hanging out near the guards."

Jonah headed toward Alexei's room, and the other two went back toward the guards' office.

I'll pull Gavin away from his tracer, and maybe he'll be so grateful to get away from the pain that he'll tell me all sorts of things, Jonah thought. *That is, unless he's lying to us about not needing immediate medical care, and even as Gavin he's in a lot of pain.*

But when Jonah stepped into Alexei's room, the boy's bed was empty. Instead, Alexei was lying on his stomach on the floor with another boy, playing with the vast lineup of toy soldiers.

"Boom!" Alexei shouted. "My cannon fire just knocked out your front ranks!"

He reached out and scattered the first two lines of soldiers on the opposite side.

"And my artillery just killed your left flank!" the other boy responded, upending twenty or thirty of Alexei's men.

"Leonid, you can't kill that many people at once," Alexei complained, setting most of his men back into place.

"How do you know?" the other boy asked.

"Because I'm the tsarevitch, and you're just a kitchen boy," Alexei said. He paused, then added, "I know people *say* that I'm not the tsarevitch anymore and that I'll never be tsar, but they're wrong. You'll see."

The other boy didn't say anything, but just lay there watching Alexei cheat.

Jonah couldn't remember ever playing with toy soldiers like this—well, who would want to in the twenty-first century, when there were video games to play instead? And anyhow, his mom had always kind of had a hang-up about letting him play games that involved pretend guns and killing people. But it seemed like Leonid and Alexei were acting like seven- or eight-year-olds, and they both looked a lot older than that. Leonid had the beginnings of dark beard stubble along his jaw—was he fifteen? Sixteen? *Seventeen?* It was even harder to tell how old Alexei was, since he was so thin and seemed to be in such constant pain. But Gavin and his tracer seemed about the same height, so Alexei must be at least thirteen.

Oh, wait, didn't Katherine and I see a birth year listed for Alexei on the Internet? Jonah wondered. *Nineteen-oh . . . something.*

That didn't help.

Alexei stretched to reach the last soldier. He gritted his teeth, as if this simple movement took incredible effort. Or caused incredible pain.

"I'll help you advance your men in the next battle," Leonid offered.

Oh, Jonah thought, watching the older boy's face. *Leonid is just humoring Alexei. Like a babysitter or something. He wouldn't be playing with toy soldiers on his own.*

Alexei looked up at Leonid, and for the first time since coming back into this room, Jonah saw a glow of tracer light.

"You're a good friend, Leonid," Alexei said. "You've been very loyal, both at Tobolsk and here in Ekaterinburg. When you leave today, you should . . . should take half of my soldiers with you. They belong to you now."

This was completely different from whatever Alexei had said in original time. Jonah could tell by the sudden burst of tracer lights around his mouth.

"And then I'll have to carry them back and forth when we play again tomorrow?" Leonid complained, creating his own glow of tracer lights.

Tomorrow, Jonah thought. *Alexei knows they won't be playing toy soldiers together tomorrow. Because, thanks to Gavin's memories, he knows when everybody is supposed to die.*

Did this also mean that Alexei—and Gavin—had given up on fighting fate?

NINETEEN

Jonah found that he couldn't bear to stay in this dim room anymore, watching teenagers play with toy soldiers like little kids. Anyhow, as long as Leonid was around, there was no way Jonah could pull Gavin out of his tracer and interrogate him.

Jonah backed out of the room. He was surprised to find that Anastasia and her two oldest sisters—Olga and Tatiana, if he remembered right—had moved their sewing projects into their own bedroom. They sat awkwardly in a circle on the floor, pushing needles in and out of piles of frilly girl clothes.

Corsets? Jonah wondered. His knowledge of old-fashioned women's clothing didn't go much further than "dress" and "skirt," so he was kind of proud of himself for coming up with the other word.

Oooh, he realized. *Maybe that's why they're in here sewing now, instead of out in the other room with their father. Maybe there's some rule about not working on clothes like that around men. Like, maybe it's considered underwear?*

"Do you have all your medicines arranged properly?" one of the older sisters asked Anastasia.

"Yes, Tatiana," Anastasia said with a knowing grin. "All arranged and secure as soon as I finish here."

Jonah couldn't understand. Medicines? Was Anastasia sick somehow too?

He stepped forward, and the floorboard squeaked beneath his foot.

All three girls glanced up, giving off tiny bursts of tracer light. Olga and Tatiana looked down again immediately, as if they thought they'd just imagined the noise. But Anastasia—or Daniella, really—met Jonah's eye. This made sense: He was still completely invisible to her sisters, of course, but she could see his translucent outline because she'd traveled through time.

Medicines? he mouthed at Daniella/Anastasia. *What medicines?*

Holding her hand off to the side where the sisters couldn't see, Daniella bent and unbent her finger at Jonah, signaling, *Come here.*

Jonah went and knelt beside her, his ear close to her mouth.

"We're sewing all our jewels into our camisoles, just in case," Daniella whispered. "We call it 'arranging our medicines' as a code so the guards don't know what we're doing. There's probably several million dollars' worth of diamonds in my lap right now. Is that . . . is that something that could be useful, do you think? For bribing someone when we all escape?"

Jonah shrugged, and turned his head so his mouth was next to her ear.

"Don't worry about that," he said. "We'll figure out what to do. I'm going to catch up with Chip and Katherine now, okay?"

Daniella nodded.

"Did you say something, Anastasia?" the third sister, Olga, asked.

"Oh, just humming," Daniella said. Or, no—Jonah should think of her as Anastasia again, since she had completely joined with her tracer once more.

"Music. What a splendid idea. Let's all sing together," Olga suggested. She began in a clear, beautiful voice, "With the saints give rest, O Christ, to the soul of your servant, where there is neither pain, nor sorrow, nor suffering . . ."

Jonah shivered, without quite knowing why.

"Can't we sing something else besides the prayer for the dead?" Anastasia asked.

"It's what I feel most like singing right now," Olga said.

Jonah backed away to watch the two sisters staring each other down: Olga pale and gaunt and as distant as if she were already dead, Anastasia flushed and little-girl perturbed and very much alive.

Still, a moment later all three sisters began singing together: "With the saints, give rest, O Christ . . ."

Jonah tiptoed out of the room.

He made his way through the empty dining room and the smoky living room. The tsar was smoking yet another cigarette; the tsarina was staring off into space as Maria read to her from the Bible.

Jonah went on into the guards' section of the house, and into the office. He had to maneuver past a cluster of guards lounging around the doorway, but the office itself had cleared out. Only Chip and Katherine were in there now. Katherine was standing beside a huge desk with papers spread over the top, poking at them in a way that made Jonah remember how challenging it had been to look through Albert Einstein's papers on their last trip through time.

"This is useless," she muttered as Jonah walked past.

He kept going, to the spot where Chip was leaning out one of the two office windows. After the smoke-filled living room and all the claustrophobic, dim rooms with whitewashed windows, Jonah was just overjoyed to see an open window. He stopped beside Chip and put his head out the window as well.

"That was quick," Chip whispered. "Did you find out anything good?"

"No," Jonah whispered back. He explained why he hadn't been able to ask Gavin a single question. He decided not to mention Alexei giving his toys away or Anastasia and her sisters singing a song about death. It all seemed too creepy. Even sewing the jewels into the clothes seemed like it could be a hopeless thing to do—intended to make sure that the jewels would be buried with the Romanovs' bodies, more than anything else.

Jonah focused on the view ahead of him. By craning his neck, he could just barely see over the wooden fence surrounding the house. And beyond it was . . .

Another wooden fence.

How paranoid are these guards that they had to put up two tall fences to hold in four girls, a sick old woman in a wheelchair, a defenseless old man, and a boy who's in too much pain to walk? Jonah wondered.

"Can you see anything past the fences?" Jonah asked Chip. Chip had had a growth spurt after coming back from the 1400s, and now he was a couple inches taller than Jonah.

"There's a church steeple over there where someone's set up . . . well, my military knowledge isn't much good in this time period, but I think that'd be a good place to stash a man with a bow and arrows," Chip said. "Looks to me like they've got a sniper's nest there with—would it be machine guns? Do they have machine guns in 1918?"

Jonah stood on his tiptoes and squinted, but it did no good.

"What are the snipers aiming at?" Jonah asked.

"This house," Chip said. He tilted his head, as if that would help him figure out angles. "Looks like the main gun is pointed at the bedroom where Alexei is right now. Did you notice there were other beds in there? And it's the nicest bedroom? I think that's where the parents sleep. So someone could be planning to assassinate the tsar in his own room."

Chip had spent two and a half years steeped in the bloodthirsty 1400s, so he was able to say that almost casually. But Jonah had to tell himself, *Katherine said the Romanovs were killed in that basement, not in their beds. So there's no danger to anyone as long as we're hanging out on this second floor.*

Of course, if he and Chip and Katherine thought they could alter fate and time to save the Romanovs' lives, wasn't it possible to alter the place where everyone was killed?

Or even who got killed?

Jonah pulled his head back into the office. The fresh air was no longer any comfort.

Chip pulled back from the window as well.

"I'm no expert on twentieth-century warfare, but doesn't it sound like there's some kind of battle going on not too far away from here?" Chip asked. "Maybe over in those mountains?"

Jonah listened. Now he could hear distant booms.

"Artillery fire," he said, repeating the words he'd heard Alexei and Leonid say in their game. "Cannons."

"Is the Russian Revolution still going on, or is that just World War One?" Chip asked.

It felt almost comical not to know the answer.

Katherine came over to the side of the desk nearest the window, so she could join the conversation.

"I think it's soldiers fighting their way here, to come and rescue the Romanovs," she said. "Maybe we just have to make sure the family stays alive an extra day or two, and then their army will save them."

It was amazing that Katherine could still look for the happiest possibility. But Jonah knew it was also ridiculous.

"Oh, yeah?" Jonah argued. "And how are we supposed to keep them alive for that extra day or two? Remember, the Elucidator's no good, and the guards all have three or four weapons apiece, and anyhow it sounds like some of the Romanovs don't even *want* to be saved . . ."

"We can make them all invisible," Katherine said.

Jonah stared at her. Chip was the expert in military strategy—well, 1400s-style—but somehow it was Katherine who'd come up with a plan.

Chip seemed to be taking her idea seriously.

"We already know the Elucidator can do that much," he said. He stroked his chin thoughtfully. Back in the 1400s he'd gotten old enough to actually have a little facial hair, and he seemed to have forgotten that he'd lost it when he went back to being thirteen. He just looked silly now. But Katherine was still gazing at him adoringly.

"You're talking about doing this at the last possible moment, so we do the least amount of damage to time, right?" Chip asked.

"Yeah, and so the Romanovs will trust us, because they'll see they don't have a choice," Katherine said.

Jonah could think of a lot of problems with this plan— how would they know when the "last possible moment" arrived? Even if they made the tsarina invisible, what would they do about her needing a wheelchair? How would the Romanovs react to suddenly being invisible? What would the guards do? How could Jonah and Chip and Katherine possibly make an entire royal family invisible without ruining time?

Jonah was just trying to figure out which argument to use first when Katherine clutched his arm and pointed warningly behind him. Jonah turned around. He'd had his back to the door, and now he saw that a uniformed man was walking into the office. Behind him all the loitering guards had snapped to attention.

"Commander Yurovsky!" they cried. "Sir!"

Yurovsky breezed past them into the office. Another officer followed him and shut the door. Jonah, Chip, and Katherine squeezed themselves over against the wall, trying to stay out of the way. But it didn't matter. Yurovsky and the other officer stopped beside the desk.

"We sent the telegram to Lenin," Yurovsky said.

Katherine dug her elbow into Jonah's side.

I think that's the leader of Russia now! Katherine mouthed at him.

Jonah frowned and nodded.

The officer with Yurovsky actually took a step back.

"What exactly did the telegram say?" he asked.

Yurovsky wasn't looking at the other man. He was gazing out the window, even though the only thing he might possibly see was the double row of wooden fences.

"It said we can't wait any longer," he said. "We can't put this off another day."

"Then it's tonight," the other officer said.

Jonah staggered back against the wall. It was one thing to read on a computer screen about an entire family being slaughtered on a date almost a hundred years earlier. It was another thing to stand three feet away from the killers as they planned for that slaughter.

Katherine gripped his arm. She was hurriedly translating for Chip, since he didn't know Russian. In an instant, his face took on the same grim expression as Katherine's. Then they both moved in close, their heads touching Jonah's.

"What about my plan?" Katherine half whispered, half mouthed, the sound barely reaching Jonah's ears.

Chip peeled back the edge of his jeans pocket, showing just the barest glimpse of the toy-soldier Elucidator's metal base.

"Think we should use this or not?" Chip asked, just as quietly.

Jonah stared at his see-through sister and his see-through friend, so grateful for the invisibility that protected them from the killers nearby and all the guards lurking beyond with their overload of guns and grenades and bayonets. How could he and Chip and Katherine *not* try to share that invisibility with the Romanovs, to save their lives?

All the arguments he'd thought of before seemed like nothing.

"We'll do it," he whispered back. "We have to."

TWENTY

When Jonah focused on Yurovsky and the other man again, they were bending over the desk, discussing details.

"Collect all the guns from the exterior guards this evening," Yurovsky was saying. "The execution squad may need the extras. And that team we've got on exterior duty spent the most time with the family. We can't be sure of their loyalties."

Possible allies! Jonah thought. *Or at least men who won't work too hard searching for the Romanovs if they hear that they've escaped.*

Jonah looked at Chip and Katherine. Katherine had done a quick translation this time, and they seemed to be thinking the same thing as Jonah. Katherine's eyebrows were raised so high they were practically up to her hairline, and Chip was almost grinning.

"Now, come with me to inspect the cellar," Yurovsky

added. "The guards' story about vagrants escaping is disturbing."

"Don't you think that was just an excuse? An outright lie?" the other man said. "I say we interrogate all the guards involved, then—"

"We don't have time for that," Yurovsky interrupted impatiently. "Let's just make sure the cellar is secure. That's all that matters right now. We can't have anyone escaping tonight."

Both men walked back out of the office.

"He's worried about vagrants escaping from the cellar?" Katherine whispered, translating again for Chip. "Does he mean Jonah and me?"

"Has to be," Chip whispered back.

Jonah looked toward the desk.

"But they didn't leave any tracers behind, so they would have left the office at this moment anyhow," he said. "One of us needs to follow them and see what they do and what they're saying."

"I'll go," Katherine said.

"I'll head down that way, too, and see if I can figure out the best route for getting the Romanovs away from the guards once they're invisible," Chip said.

Jonah wondered if Chip was just partly trying to make sure he could protect Katherine if he needed to. But Jonah wasn't going to ask about it in front of his sister.

"Then I'll go tell Alexei and Anastasia—I mean, Gavin and Daniella—what we're planning," Jonah said.

He crossed back over to the Romanovs' side of the house. The scene in the living room seemed to have barely changed: The tsar was still smoking; Maria was still reading the Bible to her mother. Olga, Tatiana, and Anastasia were still sewing in their bedroom. But when Jonah slipped past through the doorway into Alexei's room, he found the boy alone again, lying across his bed and staring up at the ceiling.

Jonah eased the bedroom door all the way shut, hoping that anyone who saw the movement from the outside would think that Alexei had done that himself. Then Jonah went over to the bed and gently tugged Gavin away from his tracer.

"Oof," Gavin said, shaking out his arms and legs. Woozily, he sat down on the edge of the bed. He rubbed his forehead.

"Are you okay?" Jonah asked.

"Better than him," Gavin said, gesturing back toward the ghostly tracer behind him. "Or, I don't know. I don't have the *pain* he lives with all the time, but—"

"So you're not having that—what's it called? Internal bleeding?—the way you thought?" Jonah asked, easing down onto the end of the bed. This could be a long conversation.

"Don't worry about it, okay?" Gavin said, just as snarly as he'd been every other time anyone had asked about it. But then his face softened. "I'm sorry. It's just . . . that doesn't matter as much as some other things right now. Really. It's not a big deal."

His voice was almost gentle now.

Whoa, Jonah thought. *What's gotten into Gavin?*

"Yeah, about some of those other things . . . ," Jonah began.

"In a minute," Gavin said. "I want to tell you what a brave kid that is." He pointed at his tracer again. "Sure, in some ways he's a spoiled brat, but when you think about what he puts up with, day in and day out . . . If I die here and you get out, will you tell people how great Alexei was?"

"You're not going to die," Jonah said.

Gavin fixed his gaze on the wall.

"One thirty in the morning," he said. "Commander Yurovsky is going to wake up our friend Dr. Botkin and tell him that our whole family needs to move out of this house because the fighting is getting too close. They're going to herd us all down to the cellar and tell us to wait there. And then the execution squad is going to shoot us all."

"But—," Jonah began.

"Isn't that what you and Katherine saw online?" Gavin asked. "Isn't that what I guaranteed would happen when I trusted Gary and Hodge and set things in motion to come back here?"

Jonah wanted to ask a little more about Gary and Hodge and how all of that had worked. But even more than that, he wanted to tell Gavin he was wrong.

"It doesn't matter what Katherine and I saw online," Jonah argued. "Because right now, that's still the future, and nothing's guaranteed about the future! Anything could happen in the next twenty-four hours! Anything!"

He wanted so badly to believe that himself.

"But only one possible future *will* happen," Gavin said. "And that's the one where I die."

Jonah was so furious at Gavin now that he couldn't sit still. He got up and paced, accidentally kicking aside some of the toy soldiers lined up on the floor. He squinted down at them. Tracer toy soldiers stood in the place of the metal figures he'd knocked aside, and in the place of the entire opposing army—an army's worth of soldiers that Alexei had given to his friend Leonid.

"Look!" Jonah said, pointing down at the soldiers. "Right there I changed something! And you changed something too, giving Leonid all those toy soldiers! Alexei didn't do that in original time!"

"He would have if he'd known he was going to die tonight," Gavin said. "If he'd known he was never going to see Leonid again. It's not like I *changed* things, exactly. It's more like I fixed things to the way they should have gone. It's like . . . improving on original time. Like time itself wants something different. Don't you feel it? I think those are the only things you can do anything about."

Gavin's words chilled Jonah.

"Yeah, well, that's what I've been trying to tell you," Jonah said. "Chip and Katherine and I figured out how to fix everything tonight. Even though we only have a limited Elucidator, we can still use it to make your whole family invisible. And then we'll rescue you all from the guards. So *none* of you are going to die."

Gavin started to shake his head at Jonah, but then he looked toward the door and dived back into the tracer Alexei sprawled across the bed.

A split second later the door creaked open, and Tatiana stood there looking anxiously toward Alexei.

"Were you arguing with someone in here, baby?" she asked in a baffled tone.

"Just using different voices for the soldiers in my battle," Alexei said, weakly lifting his hand to gesture toward the toy army on the floor.

Both Alexei's words and his movement produced bursts

of tracer lights, so none of it was what he would have said or done in original time. Jonah peeked past Tatiana—yes, she'd left a tracer behind too. Her glowing ghostly outline still sat sewing on the floor with Anastasia and Olga. So Jonah and Gavin's argument had disturbed time.

"You're lying on the bed and playing with the soldiers halfway across the room?" Tatiana asked teasingly.

"I'm *imagining* the way the battle would go," Alexei said. "Because . . . it hurts my knee to lie on the floor for very long."

"That's some imagination you've got," Tatiana said, still in a light voice. "Looks like it took out these brave men." She pointed at the soldiers Jonah had kicked. "Want me to set them back up so they can fight another day?"

"Sure," Alexei said. "Sounds like a good idea."

Tatiana walked over and picked up the toppled soldiers. This was her native time, so of course she couldn't see any of the toys' tracers, any more than she could see invisible time travelers.

And yet she put every single toy soldier back in the exact same place as its tracer.

TWENTY-ONE

That's not fate, Jonah told himself. *It's not destiny. It doesn't have anything to do with our chances for saving the Romanovs tonight.*

Why did he feel like he was just trying to fool himself?

He reminded himself that he'd seen the same phenomenon—where tracers seemed to be pulling time back to its original path—in 1600 and in 1611, and yet his enemy Second Chance had been able to dramatically reshape time in those years and split it into a totally new direction.

Yeah, and he almost ruined time completely, Jonah reminded himself.

Second was not exactly the best role model.

Jonah got disgusted with himself for thinking in circles so much. He backed out of Alexei's room and turned around to see if it was a good time to talk to Anastasia/Daniella.

She was still sitting on the floor with Tatiana's tracer

and the flesh-and-blood Olga, but she seemed to have abandoned her sewing. A camisole still lay in her lap, but she was using it to play a game with one of the small dogs Jonah had seen in the living room area before.

"Peekaboo, Jimmy!" Anastasia cried, pulling the camisole over and then away from the dog's face. "Get it, Olga? Peekaboo, and he's a Pekingese?"

She laughed like this was the most hilarious joke ever. And the thing was, even though it was a really stupid play on words, he still had to hold back a chuckle. Anastasia was just one of those people you wanted to laugh with, no matter what.

Then something else hit him.

Peekaboo, Pekingese—that was English! Wasn't it? Did Daniella just totally mess up and forget that Anastasia should be speaking Russian? Jonah wondered.

He quickly bent down beside Daniella/Anastasia and whispered in her ear, "What are you doing? Anastasia wouldn't speak English to her sisters!"

Holding the camisole up to block her own face, Daniella separated from her tracer to whisper back, "Yes, she would! We've always spoken English a lot, because Mama prefers that to Russian . . . even the servants understand it!"

Okay, then, Jonah thought. *But what kind of royalty prefers a different language than their own country's?*

He decided that wasn't something he could worry about right now. He watched Daniella rejoin her tracer completely again. Now Anastasia was draping the camisole over the dog's back like a cape.

"Anastasia, that camisole is going to smell like dog," Olga said disapprovingly.

"Oh, good," Anastasia said, dipping down to rub her face against the dog's fur. "I love the way Jimmy smells."

Even grim-faced Olga laughed at that, probably proving that Anastasia had an amazing future ahead of her as a comedian.

If we can make sure she lives through the night, Jonah thought.

He leaned in closer to Anastasia once again. The camisole had slipped over her face, as well as the dog's, so Jonah thought he could talk to her without Olga noticing.

"We have a plan," Jonah whispered in Anastasia/Daniella's ear. "When . . . when the danger comes tonight, we're going to use the Elucidator to make your whole family invisible. And then we'll all escape. Chip is figuring out the best escape route now."

At first Jonah wasn't sure that she'd heard him, because she didn't move. The camisole stayed draped over her head. But then she leaned her head back a little and motioned for him to put his ear near her mouth.

"You can't just save my family," she whispered. "If the guards threaten any of our servants and friends, you have to make them invisible and save them, too."

Jonah felt dizzy.

"How many people are we talking about here?" he whispered back.

Anastasia started listing them off on her fingers.

"One, Dr. Botkin, who's been so good at taking care of Mama and Alexei," she began. "Two—"

"Anastasia, what are you muttering about over there?" Olga asked.

Anastasia raised her head.

"I'm telling Jimmy all the people who have been loyal to us," she said. "He's just a dog. Sometimes he forgets who he should avoid biting."

"Jimmy wouldn't bite anybody," Olga said, all but rolling her eyes. "He's too lazy."

Still, Anastasia's excuse made it possible for her to finish the list out loud. She cupped the dog's face in her hands and acted like she was talking only to him.

"Two, Anna Demidova, Mama's maid, who's built like an ocean liner—"

"Anastasia! You shouldn't say things like that!" Olga cried, acting scandalized.

"It's true, though, isn't it?" Anastasia asked mischievously.

"Three, Papa's footman, Alexei Trupp. Four, our cook, Ivan Kharitonov."

So many people! Jonah thought. *It's going to be hard enough just rescuing the five Romanovs, and now Anastasia wants us to add four more people to the list?*

But Anastasia wasn't done yet.

"And five," she added, "the kitchen boy, Leonid Sednev, who's willing to play toy soldiers with Alexei for hours and hours and hours when all the rest of us are sick of it."

Jonah squinted at Anastasia/Daniella.

"Leonid?" he asked her in a whisper. "But Alexei acted like he was never going to see that kid again. He said—"

"What?" she whispered back.

"Never mind," Jonah said. It all seemed too complicated to try to explain in a series of whispers.

"Do you promise to save all of those people too?" Daniella hissed.

Jonah sighed.

"We'll do our best," he said. "But when the time comes, you and Gavin will have to keep everyone calm, and tell them where to go . . ."

When Chip figures it out, he thought. *If saving the Romanovs is even possible.*

He realized that he'd forgotten to watch for tracer lights while Anastasia/Daniella was listing the names.

Maybe in original time Anastasia really had been instructing Jimmy on who was loyal and who he should bite.

So without Chip and Katherine and me, the Romanovs' only defenses would have been Maria's flirting, Anastasia's jokes, and the teeth of a little Pekingese dog? Jonah thought. *No wonder they were doomed.*

And then he wanted to take that word back, censor his own thoughts.

Jonah wished he could just talk to Anastasia alone—or rather Daniella, pulled completely away from her tracer—but that wasn't possible as long as Olga was sitting there. He drifted back out into the dining room and on into the living room again. A tall, bearded man with gold-rimmed glasses was now sitting beside the tsar, and they were playing some sort of card game.

The doctor, maybe? Jonah guessed. The man looked almost as sickly as the tsarina.

"And that's trump," he said, laying down a card. "I win."

"Ah, well, it's time for supper anyhow," the tsar said, gathering up the whole pile of cards and arranging them in a precise stack, all the corners lined up perfectly.

Does he know what's coming? Jonah wondered.

He couldn't understand how the tsar could sit there so calmly straightening cards if he had even a suspicion that the guards were right now plotting to kill his entire family.

Maria had said the family had been held prisoner in this house for seventy-eight days. Maybe they just automatically assumed that there would be a seventy-ninth day, and an eightieth . . . and on and on and on.

The doctor and the tsar moved toward the dining room table, and the rest of the Romanovs joined them: the tsarina grimacing as she rolled her wheelchair forward, Alexei limping out of his room, the girls silently helping their mother and brother into place.

"Eggs!" Alexei exclaimed, peering down at the platter before him as if this was a huge treat.

"Just for you," his mother said fondly. "The nuns who brought the supplies today know what you need to grow up big and strong."

Jonah winced at that. Alexei was so sickly and pale and weak that it seemed cruel even to use the words "big and strong" around him.

But the entire family beamed at him as if they all believed it would happen.

Delusional, Jonah thought. *Every single one of them. Or . . . just good actors trying to keep a sick boy happy?*

He couldn't decide.

The Romanovs sang a blessing for their food. This wasn't a quick mumbling before digging in, like most of the blessings Jonah had said in his life back home. The family seemed truly grateful to have any food at all, and they truly seemed to believe that God would take care of them.

Oh, God, he thought, almost a prayer of his own. *Is that true? Or are we fighting against you, trying to keep this family alive tonight? Why would you want them dead?*

Jonah had talked with his favorite time agent, JB, about the connection between God and fate and destiny and original time, and he still didn't understand it. Jonah's argument, the last time he'd seen JB, had been that you should just help other people, no matter what.

And that's what Chip and Katherine and I are going to try to do tonight, he told himself.

The family sat eating crude black bread and a thin soup and—in Alexei's case—eggs. Anastasia told jokes and did an imitation of the cook chopping onions that made everyone laugh.

And she can do that, even knowing what the guards are planning for tonight, Jonah thought. *She knows. Alexei knows. Maria may not know that it's tonight, but she knows that it's a distinct possibility, anytime. Probably everyone at the table knows as much as Maria does. And they can still laugh?*

He couldn't decide: Were they incredibly noble and brave, sitting there eating and laughing like a normal family on a normal night, pretending for everyone else's sake that everything was fine? Or were they idiots for not jumping up and plotting and scheming and doing everything they could to escape?

Halfway through the supper, Jonah saw the door to the guards' section of the house come open. Commander Yurovsky stepped through it.

"Citizens," Yurovsky said, standing at the threshold of the dining room, "I apologize for disturbing your meal, but I have news to share."

Jonah saw everyone at the table tense and dart glances at one another. And then, just as quickly, they all seemed to try to act normal.

"What is it?" the tsarina asked imperiously.

"Your kitchen boy will be leaving this evening. His uncle Ivan has come back into town and asked to spend some time with young Leonid," Yurovsky said.

"What? *No,*" the tsarina exploded. "This is the fifth servant that you've taken from us, and not a single one has come back. And Leonid is such a fine playmate for Alexei. What will Alexei do without him?"

Jonah looked at Alexei, who looked much less surprised than the rest of the family.

Because he knew this would happen too, Jonah thought. *When he was back in the twenty-first century, he must have read up on how everything happens with Leonid, too. And that's how he knew to give Leonid those toy soldiers this afternoon.*

"Oh, I assure you, this time the boy will come back," Yurovsky said smoothly. Jonah didn't know how anybody sitting at the table could believe him. "Why would you want to deny the boy a chance to spend time with his own family?"

Yurovsky turned to go back toward his own office. Dr. Botkin and Tatiana both bolted from the table and followed him, arguing the whole way.

"Why does Ivan not come to see the boy here?" Dr. Botkin asked as they stepped past Jonah.

"Couldn't this visit be arranged another time?" Tatiana asked, right behind him.

Jonah considered following along—until he noticed that Chip and Katherine had stepped back into the living room. He went over to stand by them.

"I heard the guards say that Leonid's uncle isn't even alive anymore," Katherine muttered angrily. "This is just an excuse to get the kitchen boy away from here. So he doesn't have to die with everyone else."

"Why do they care about that one boy, and not the other servants?" Jonah asked.

"Oh, it's not because they actually *care*," Chip said.

"They just don't want to have to deal with as many bodies after they kill everyone," Katherine added, her face twisted in disgust. "Ugh! I hate those people! They talk about bodies like they're . . . they're garbage. Not even human beings. And then Yurovsky can stand there talking to the Romanovs, looking them right in the eye—"

"Shh," Jonah whispered, because Katherine, in her fury, was getting too loud. "They'll hear you in the dining room."

"What if they did?" Katherine asked, still whispering, but only barely. "What if I went over there and asked the Elucidator to make me visible and then told the Romanovs everything the guards have planned?"

"If you did that," Chip whispered back calmly, "they'd panic and scream and then the guards would come and shoot them right away, instead of waiting until it's dark and they think no one will hear. And that would ruin the plans *we've* put together. Okay?"

Katherine pursed her lips. When she spoke again, it was a whisper once more.

"I hate this too," she said. "I hate not being able to tell them what's going on, and I hate having to stay invisible, and I hate not having a better plan or a better Elucidator . . ."

Chip put his arm around Katherine's shoulder.

"I hate all that too," he said. "But now that you've gotten that off your chest, can't we focus on what we need to do right now?"

"Okay," Katherine said sulkily.

Just then Dr. Botkin and Tatiana came out of the guards' section and went back to the table.

"Yurovsky gave us his word that this won't be like the other times servants left," Dr. Botkin announced in a soothing voice. "Leonid will be back. Everything will be fine."

Even the tsarina looked at him placidly and smiled and went back to chewing.

But did anybody sitting at the table actually believe him? Did he even believe himself?

TWENTY-TWO

Jonah and Katherine and Chip told one another everything they'd witnessed and figured out since they'd gone
in different directions. By then the Romanovs were finished with their supper.

"What?" Katherine asked Jonah in surprise. "You're not
scurrying over there to eat their leftovers?"

Jonah had been starving in practically every single
time period he'd ever visited. In 1903 he'd eaten scraps
from Albert Einstein's table and from abandoned plates
in railroad-station restaurants. In 1600 he'd eaten what
seemed like an ocean's worth of fish. In 1483 he'd eaten
hard crusts of bread and wished for pizza or lasagna.

But somehow he couldn't even think about food right
now.

"Not hungry," he mumbled.

Katherine nodded.

"Got it," she said. "Neither am I."

"Sometimes it's better not to eat before a battle," Chip agreed.

He's thinking of what lies ahead as a battle? Jonah wondered.

That made Jonah feel even worse.

The entire Romanov family began moving back into the living room. Jonah, Chip, and Katherine followed Anastasia/Daniella and Alexei/Gavin and, in hasty whispers, tried to fill them in as much as they could on the exact details of the plan. Chip had figured out which gate the whole group could walk through once they were invisible; he'd also scouted out an empty shed nearby where the whole group could rest and decide their next step.

"Why don't you just make us all invisible *now?*" Daniella asked, hiding her words as she bent over to pick up some unfinished needlepoint. "None of us are doing anything important to history, as far as I can tell."

It appeared that she was right. The whole family was settling back into more listless card-playing, reading, and sewing. They were just passing time.

But Jonah whispered back, "We can't know for sure. We don't want to damage time any more than we have to. And anyway, Chip says we've got a better chance of getting away if we're outdoors when we turn everyone invisible. The guards will have to take everyone outside to get them to the basement, because there's only that one door."

He couldn't explain anything else because Maria leaned too close to Anastasia just then, asking, "Do you think I've hemmed this skirt well enough, or should I tear out this section and start again?"

She held up a threadbare black skirt. It looked like she was moving the hem to hide the spots where the fabric had worn thin.

Wish it were that easy to fix time, Jonah thought. *I'd like to start again with this whole trip—with a fully working Elucidator. And with open communications with JB, so he could tell us the best way to handle all of this. . . .*

Except—*would* Jonah want that? Wouldn't JB disapprove of this plan every bit as much as he'd disapproved of some of the things Jonah had done in 1903? And hadn't it turned out then that Jonah was right and JB was wrong?

Oh, God, you *approve of what we're planning, don't you?* Jonah prayed again.

Jonah's parents had taken him and Katherine to church their whole lives, but for his first thirteen years Jonah had never thought deeply about anything connected to religion.

Time travel had changed all that.

But for all the thinking I've done, shouldn't I be more sure that I'm right? Jonah thought. *More sure that we're doing the right thing now?*

Jonah was driving himself crazy. He moved over beside Chip and tugged his friend into an isolated corner of the dining room.

"Isn't there anything else I can do right now, besides just talking and thinking?" he asked. "Wouldn't it help if I went down to the yard and, I don't know, built a booby trap or something to take out as many guards as I can before tonight?"

"Oh, yeah, great idea," Chip said sarcastically. "That wouldn't put the guards on alert, or make them change their plans—which would throw off our plans. . . . Anyhow, how are you going to build a booby trap in just four hours?"

"We've still got four hours to pass with nothing to do?" Jonah groaned.

"Talk to the Romanovs," Chip said. "They've been waiting here for seventy-eight days with nothing to do."

Jonah looked toward the living room. Anastasia was now down on the floor, playing with all three dogs. Olga had joined the card-playing with her father and Dr. Botkin. Tatiana was taking her turn reading Bible verses to her mother. Maria was reading with Alexei, with Katherine hovering translucently nearby, looking frustrated because

Maria had cut off any chance for Katherine to whisper some more in Alexei's ear. Katherine was bouncing up and down, jittery with impatience.

She couldn't last through seventy-eight days of doing nothing, Jonah thought. *And neither could I.*

Now Jonah saw the Romanovs' calm blandness in a different light yet again. He still couldn't decide if they were noble and brave or total delusional idiots. But they were definitely very patient people. And . . . nice. How else could they have they managed to stay cooped up together for so long without killing one another? Or at least arguing constantly?

The Romanovs stayed peaceful. They just calmly traded around who was reading and who was playing cards. When the grandfather clock in the corner of the living room area chimed ten, they gathered for evening prayers with Dr. Botkin and the servants. Then they began heading for bed.

"Maybe we should try to get some sleep too," Chip whispered to Jonah. "So we're fresh and alert when the time comes."

"*I* couldn't sleep," Jonah said.

"Me neither," Katherine agreed, joining them in their secluded corner of the dining room.

It seemed that Dr. Botkin had the same problem. Long

after the Romanovs and their servants disappeared into their bedrooms and turned out the lights, he stayed up writing. Jonah tiptoed over and peeked over the doctor's shoulder. He was adding more to a letter that seemed to have been started a few weeks ago, addressed to someone named Alexander Botkin—a brother? A son? Dr. Botkin had his hand over a large section of the letter, but Jonah read the portion he could see:

I don't think I am fated to write again . . . my voluntary confinement here is not so much limited by time as it is limited by my earthly existence. In essence, I am already dead, dead for my children, for my friends, for my work . . .

He knows, Jonah thought. *He knows what's coming.*

What if that was all that was required for fate to take over—everyone expecting his life to go a certain way?

Or to *end* a certain way?

TWENTY-THREE

Jonah actually did doze off, because there was nothing else to do. He awoke to the sound of a ringing bell. In the darkness it took him a moment to remember where he was, and by then Dr. Botkin had a light on and was struggling his way out of a makeshift bed in the corner of the living room.

"I'm coming, I'm coming," he muttered, shuffling over to open the door to the guards' section of the house. "What's wrong?"

Commander Yurovsky stood on the other side of the door.

"The fighting's getting close," he said. "We don't have much time. If the White Army attacks the city, it won't be safe up here on the top floor. When the artillery hits, when the bullets are flying . . ."

Dr. Botkin stared silently at Yurovsky. Jonah couldn't tell if the doctor was hiding terror or hope. Maybe he wanted the battle to come into the city?

"So everyone needs to go down to the cellar to be safe," Yurovsky continued. "And then I'm ordering a truck to move the family somewhere else. Will you let them know?"

"Yes," Dr. Botkin said curtly. He shuffled away to tap at bedroom doors. Yurovsky went back to his office.

Jonah rubbed his eyes. His back was stiff from sleeping hunched over against the living-room wall, but he could feel the nervous energy zinging back.

"That's just wrong, him saying that everyone has to go down to the cellar to be 'safe,' when really that's where they're going to die," Katherine whispered, waking up indignant.

She and Jonah quickly told Chip everything Yurovsky had said.

"Yurovsky is good at lying," Chip whispered back. He tilted his head. "But I think part of what he said is true. I think maybe the fighting really *is* getting closer."

Jonah listened too. At first he thought he was just hearing thunder, but there were too many booms, too close together.

"The White Army—whoever that is—if they're coming

to attack this city, does that mean that maybe they're on the same side of the war as the Romanovs?" Jonah asked.

"I bet they are," Katherine said. "And I bet they're coming to rescue the whole family. Well, after we rescue them first."

And if this army puts the tsar back on the throne of Russia when he's supposed to be dead—wouldn't that change a lot of things in history? Jonah wondered.

"Things won't get that far," Jonah said, to reassure himself as much as to argue against Katherine. "As soon as time agents see that we've saved the Romanovs' lives, someone like JB will come and pick us all up. So we don't change 1918 too much, but the whole family gets to live. In the future, I mean."

This type of plan had worked out before in connection with some of Jonah's other trips through time. But it seemed riskier now. Somehow the year 1918 felt more like a time where one change could have massive consequences.

Jonah could hear the Romanovs in their bedrooms asking one another, "Which clothes should we put on?" "Where do you think they're taking us after the cellar?" "What should we take with us?"

He even heard Anastasia's and Alexei's voices in the mix, undoubtedly just saying whatever they would have said in original time.

"It's a good thing we arranged all our 'medicines' this afternoon," Anastasia's voice rang out, a bit too loudly. "We wouldn't want to go anywhere without our 'medicines'!"

Why does she have to remind her sisters to wear their camisoles with the jewels sewn into them? Jonah wondered. *Would any of them forget?*

The clock showed that forty minutes passed before the Romanovs and their servants gathered in the living room. Jonah was amazed—it didn't feel like time was crawling now. It felt like time was zipping by, each moment bringing them closer and closer to the "do or die" beginning of Katherine's plan.

"Now," Katherine whispered.

Dr. Botkin was opening the door to the guards' section again. And then Jonah, Katherine, and Chip made sure they got ahead of the entire group headed for the stairs. It was Yurovsky and three guards in the lead, followed by the tsar, who was carrying Alexei. Even in the dim stairway Jonah could see Alexei grimacing with every jolt and bump.

Behind the tsar and Alexei, Olga walked with her mother, who struggled forward leaning on first a cane, then Olga's arm. The three other sisters walked behind them, and then Dr. Botkin and the servants. The giant stuffed bear and her cubs loomed ahead of the group in the shadows, and the entire family stopped and crossed themselves.

"Ah, yes, respect for the dead," Yurovsky said. "And, of course, for Russia the bear. Very nice."

For the first time Jonah heard a certain nervousness in the man's voice. Would any of the Romanovs notice it too? Or would they just think he was worried about the attack on Ekaterinburg?

Just as the family was turning to go on down the stairs, three shapes zipped out of the darkness, barking.

The family dogs.

"Joy! Jimmy! Ortipo! Down, all of you! Stay! Stay here!" Anastasia called to them.

All three of the dogs whimpered but obediently sat down.

Can't the dogs at least hear the fear in Anastasia's voice? Jonah wondered. He saw a flash of tracer light back by Anastasia: the little Pekingese's tracer squirming past the servants and leaping up into Anastasia's arms. More tracer light showed that in original time Anastasia would have cradled the dog, hugged him tight—and carried him on down the steps.

In original time she would have thought she was carrying the dog away from danger, Jonah realized. *But now she knows the dogs are safer staying here.*

The glow of the tracer lights was just bright enough that Jonah could see the tears glistening in Anastasia's eyes.

Don't look—just focus on what's working well, Jonah told himself. *The dogs wouldn't stay quiet when the time comes for us turn everyone invisible and sneak away. So they* have *to stay here.*

The tracer light kept glowing near Anastasia's arms, where they dangled free and empty instead of carrying the dog. But, tracer or real, her arms were covered with the sleeves of a simple black dress, rather than her University of Michigan sweatshirt. Jonah was glad that he and Chip and Katherine had taken the precaution of telling Gavin and Daniella to put on an extra layer of Alexei's and Anastasia's clothes, so that even apart from their tracers they would still look like their twentieth-century selves.

Not that it's going to matter once everyone's invisible, but it helps for moments like this, Jonah told himself. *See? We thought of everything. This* is *going to work!*

The entire group descended the narrow staircase. Then they walked toward the same door that Jonah, Chip, and Katherine had used to come into the house that afternoon. Jonah tensed up. The crucial moment was just ahead. He saw Chip reach into his pocket and pull out the Elucidator. Then, as the guards opened the door, Jonah, Chip, and Katherine slipped past them.

"Ready?" Jonah whispered.

Chip nodded, clutching the toy-soldier Elucidator tightly in his hand.

As soon as the tsar and Alexei stepped outside, Chip put his hand on the tsar's shoulder and bent his arm so he was touching Alexei's back as well.

"Make the tsar and Alexei invisible," Chip whispered, and spun them into the darkness behind him, in the opposite direction from the basement.

It had been Chip's idea to change only two or three people at a time, as they stepped out from the doorway. That way, he said, there'd be time to warn each person individually, before the whole group noticed all at once that their bodies had vanished and they started screaming.

Jonah could hear Alexei—or, rather, Gavin—murmuring into his father's ear: "Papa, something wonderful just happened. This is all a dream, but we're invisible now. We just have to be quiet and we can all escape."

They'd added the "this is all a dream" part because they didn't think any of the Romanovs would catch on quickly enough to the true explanation.

The tsar, at least, took the news calmly. He didn't make a sound. Maybe he was too stunned to say anything.

Chip reached for the next two Romanovs coming through the door: the tsarina and Olga. This could be a difficult pair, because the tsarina was bound to have questions, and would ask them. Loudly.

It's a good thing the tsar is taking this so quietly. Now Gavin will be able to explain to Olga and his mother, instead of Katherine or me having to do it, Jonah thought.

He glanced over his shoulder to make sure Gavin would be ready. Just then, a beam of light shone through the cracks in the wood fence—maybe from a car or truck driving by. The light fell directly on the tsar and Alexei/Gavin, glowing all around them.

But—not glowing through them. They weren't see-through. They were solid and whole and normal, a man and a boy in tunics and caps, looking just as they had before Chip called out the Elucidator command.

The invisibility hadn't worked.

TWENTY-FOUR

Alexei/Gavin must have noticed this at the same time as Jonah, because he began yelling, "It didn't work! It didn't work!"

He jumped down from his father's arms—or, rather, Gavin jumped down, suddenly appearing as a healthy, able-bodied kid with a streak of purple in his hair, but still in Alexei's tunic and pants. He grabbed Chip and yanked the Elucidator from his hands.

"Make my family invisible!" Gavin screamed. "Make my entire family invisible!"

Nothing happened.

At least, no one turned invisible.

One of the lead guards cocked a rifle in Gavin's direction. The tsarina leaped toward the gun, knocking it aside. The gun went off, but the bullet zinged uselessly out into the garden.

Somehow the tsarina was unafraid.

"See what you've done, putting my son under this strain in the middle of the night?" she accused. "You've threatened his sanity now! Alexei, baby, go back to your father. He'll take care of you! Everything will be all right. . . ."

But she was sprawled on the ground now, the guard pointing the rifle at her.

Gavin threw the Elucidator down and scrambled over to the tsarina.

"Don't shoot her," he cried.

Olga, Tatiana, and Maria raced out the door and joined Gavin by their mother's side. Tracer lights were glowing all around now: the tracer Romanovs still obediently following the tracer guards toward the basement while the real Romanovs huddled together and the real guards looked toward Yurovsky to see what they were possibly supposed to do now.

Daniella split from her Anastasia tracer as well, but dived for the toy-soldier Elucidator that Gavin had dropped.

"Make my family invisible! Make my family invisible!" she demanded. Nothing happened. She thrust the Elucidator at Jonah and Chip and Katherine and wailed, "Why won't it work now? It's like it's just an ordinary toy soldier again!"

Ordinary toy soldier, Jonah thought. *Ordinary toy soldier . . .*

He grabbed the toy soldier from Daniella's hand. In the glow of all the tracer lights, Jonah looked closely at the toy soldier: same khaki-green uniform, same fierce stance, same tilted cap, except . . . where was the tiny patch of bare metal where Gavin had chipped off the paint?

"Jonah!" Chip cried, horror racing across his face as he came to the same conclusion as Jonah. "What if I picked up the wrong toy soldier back in Alexei's room?"

"I can find it!" Jonah cried. "I know what to look for!"

His cries got lost in the sound of all the Romanovs and the guards—and now Dr. Botkin and the servants, too—screaming and shouting and pleading. But at least no one had been shot, so maybe there was still time. . . .

Jonah shoved his way past the last servant coming out the door—the cook? The footman? The man gasped and looked instantly mystified, but Jonah figured that was the least of their worries right now. Jonah dashed back to the stairs and leaped up them three at a time. He raced to Alexei's room and hit the lights.

There on the floor, still lined up neatly, were the rows and rows of Alexei's toy soldiers. Jonah crashed down on his knees beside them. The light was too dim, and Jonah didn't have time to methodically pick each one up and examine it for a chipped patch in the painted-on cap. So instead he swept the soldiers aside, five or six at a time, and looked to make sure each one left behind a tracer.

The Elucidator wouldn't have a tracer, since it doesn't belong to this time, Jonah told himself. *So as soon as there's a toy soldier that doesn't leave a tracer, I'll know that's the right one.*

He moved fast, like a wrecking ball through Alexei's miniature army. Sweep, look, sweep, look, sweep, look . . .

In seconds all the toy soldiers were in a jumble on the floor.

And every single one of them left behind a tracer version of itself still standing and looking orderly and alert.

What? Jonah thought. *How could that be? Did I just go too fast? Did Alexei leave behind more soldiers somewhere else?*

Only then did Jonah raise his gaze beyond the piled soldiers to another grouping—not of more toy soldiers, but of their tracers. Tracers of an entire opposing army.

Jonah's memory flashed back to that afternoon, to seeing Alexei sprawled on the floor alongside Leonid, to Alexei telling the other boy, *Take half of my soldiers. They belong to you now.*

The Elucidator must have been in the group of toy soldiers Leonid took with him when he left.

And Jonah had no idea where it was now.

TWENTY-FIVE

Jonah wasted time searching back through the pile of toy soldiers, the same slow method he'd been trying to avoid. He was sure it was hopeless. But how could he go back and tell the others that *everything* was hopeless?

Chipped paint on the cap, chipped paint on the cap—please let me see chipped paint on some cap, he thought.

From outside he heard a boom.

That couldn't have been gunfire, he told himself. *I mean, not a rifle or pistol going off down in the courtyard or in the cellar. It had to be a cannon far away, off in the battle being fought in the mountains around this city. . . .*

It didn't sound far away.

Another boom reverberated, sounding even closer.

Jonah dropped the last of the useless toy soldiers to the floor and scrambled up. He lurched out the door and back through the Romanov sisters' room, through the dining room, off toward the stairs. Going down, he took the steps four at a time, careening side to side and barely staying upright. He burst out through the door.

The courtyard outside was empty now, and as far as he could tell, so was the garden beyond.

The door to the cellar was closed, but Jonah yanked it open. He didn't bother pulling it shut behind him. He did try to be a little quieter going down these steps, because he could hear voices down below.

"What? There is not even a chair to sit on down here?" the tsarina was complaining, still sounding imperious in spite of everything that had happened. "You expect us to *stand* while we wait, when my son and I are both in such pain?"

"I'll have a guard get chairs for both of you," Yurovsky said apologetically. "Aleksander?"

Jonah was close enough now that he could see a guard break off from the group and head for the stairs. Jonah had to press against the wall to avoid getting in the man's way.

"The heir wants to die sitting in a chair?" one of the other guards muttered under his breath. "Let him."

But that guard was far back from the Romanovs, so Jonah was sure that none of them heard him.

"I'll go watch for the truck, so we can get you out of here quickly," Yurovsky told the Romanovs.

"Thank you," the tsar said stiffly, as if trying to make up for his wife's rudeness.

And how can Yurovsky still act like he's helping the Romanovs, when he's planning to kill them? Jonah wondered. Another terrible thought struck him: Probably there really was a truck coming, to take away the dead bodies.

As Yurovsky headed back for the stairs, the rest of the guards stood around awkwardly, mixed in with the Romanovs and their servants. But because of tracers, Jonah could see that in original time everyone had broken off into the two separate rooms, with tracer versions of the double doors shut in between. The tracers of the guards sat against the wall of one room, checking and rechecking their weapons and nervously smoking and passing around a flask.

They seemed to be trying to get drunk.

Beyond them, in the second room, the tracer versions of the Romanovs and their servants were clustered around two tracer chairs. They almost looked as if they were posing for a professional photograph, like one of the pictures Jonah and Katherine had seen on the Internet. The tracer tsar stood in the front, with Alexei beside him in a chair and Dr. Botkin on his other side. The tsarina sat on the second chair, beside Alexei, her three oldest daughters clustered around her. Anastasia stood back with the servants, seemingly off in her own little world.

Jonah veered away from all the tracers and the clumps of people and looked frantically around for Katherine and Chip. They were standing off to the side, in the corner, see-through and out of the way.

"You found the Elucidator?" Chip whispered eagerly, holding out his hand for it.

Jonah just shook his head.

"You don't have it?" Katherine wailed.

"Leonid must have taken it away with the other toy soldiers," Jonah said.

"Then we've got to find Leonid!" Katherine exclaimed.

"How are we supposed to know where he is?" Jonah asked. "You think we can just ask Yurovsky and he'll tell us?"

Katherine opened her mouth to reply, but Jonah didn't listen. He was suddenly distracted by a burst of tracer light out in the open area of the room. Jonah could see the tracer guards springing to their feet, dropping their flasks and cigarettes. They burst through the tracer double doors, then spread out into a line in the doorway between the two rooms and began firing and firing and firing. Tracer smoke rose with the silent blasts, hiding the tracer bodies that fell: the Romanovs, Dr. Botkin, the servants.

Meanwhile, in real time, the Romanovs and their servants stood in practically the very same spots, but elbow to elbow with their would-be killers.

Jonah had to look away. Katherine grabbed his arm and made him look back at her.

"We can't let that happen for real!" she whispered fiercely. "We can't!"

"What can we do without the Elucidator?" Jonah asked.

Chip clutched his head.

"We never should have let the Romanovs be herded down here into the basement," he groaned, tugging at his own hair. "They're trapped! There's no way out!"

"Chip, you said we had to come down here!" Katherine argued. "You said those guards were looking too trigger-happy with all the arguing up in the courtyard, and everyone got so upset when we could hear the cannon fire so close by . . ."

Chip was looking down at objects on the floor. No—tracer objects.

Tracer bullets.

He touched the wall behind them, which had tracer gouges in it. Jonah saw other tracer bullets embedded in the plaster.

"If they do start firing the same way as in original time," Chip muttered, "*we* won't be safe here either. Not the way bullets bounce around. . . . Maybe we should get out of the way now."

"We can't leave Gavin and Daniella behind!" Katherine insisted.

Jonah looked around to make sure none of the real guards were ready to start firing yet. They weren't, but they had moved away from the Romanovs, into the other room. The doors stood barely cracked between the two rooms, so Jonah could see that now all the guards sat slumped to the floor, their backs against the wall. One was pulling a flask from his pocket; others were lighting up cigarettes. All of them were holding guns.

Déjà vu, Jonah thought. *They look just like their tracers did five minutes ago.*

So how much time did Jonah and his friends have before the guards started firing those guns for real? Was there any way to stop them?

The tracer versions of the guards had stopped firing, but now they carried tracer bayonets into the room with all the fallen Romanovs. In the dimming tracer smoke, Jonah could see that the tracer guards were stabbing at the tracer bodies on the floor. It looked like they feared that the flurry of bullets hadn't been enough to kill.

Wait—I guess they weren't, Jonah thought. He remembered that a tracer stopped glowing at the moment that the person would have died in original time. *But Olga's tracer is still glowing, and so is Tatiana's, and so is Maria's . . .*

He couldn't tell about Anastasia and Alexei, because both Gavin and Daniella had stayed joined to their tracers, sliding down toward the floor.

Because they feel the link to their dying tracers? Jonah wondered. *Or just because they're giving up?*

The tracer guards weren't giving up. They viciously stabbed their bayonets into one body after another; they stood inches away from the wounded tracers and shot them in the head, point-blank.

"Oh, no," Jonah moaned. "Oh, no. All those jewels the girls sewed into their clothes—they must have worked almost like bulletproof vests, letting the bullets bounce off. So their deaths are going to be even worse. Those tracers are terrified; they're screaming . . ."

He turned and walked through one tracer after another—a guard with a bayonet, the dying doctor, the dying maid—and rushed to Anastasia's side.

"Daniella!" he whispered in her ear. "We've got to pull you and Gavin out *now*! The Elucidator is missing, but somehow we'll get you out of here, somehow . . ."

"Not without the rest of my family!" Daniella whispered back through gritted teeth.

She had her hands on her hips, her hands probably

covering a fortune in diamonds and other jewels.

And what good is any of it when all those jewels are just going to ensure that she has a horrible death? Jonah wondered.

It was a shame none of those diamonds could make her invisible.

Wait—what if one of them can? Jonah wondered.

"Daniella! Please!" he hissed in her ear. "Give me one of your jewels! I can't explain, but—quick! This might save you!"

Daniella didn't ask questions. Jonah saw her separate from her tracer enough to start picking at the seam along her waist.

The guard who'd been sent out for chairs came back holding one in each hand. He clattered down the stairs. When Jonah looked up again, Alexei and the tsarina were both seated in the chairs, and somehow the other Romanovs and their servants had stepped into place around them, in the same positions their tracers had held a few minutes earlier, before the bullets started flying.

Jonah did a double take—Yurovsky was back now too.

"Daniella! Hurry!" Jonah whispered.

Outside he could hear a truck revving. The tsar said something that Jonah didn't quite catch—maybe, "Are you ready for us to get into the truck?"

"Stand up, everyone," Yurovsky demanded.

The tsarina mumbled complaints but did it anyhow; Alexei didn't move. Yurovsky went to stand directly in front of the tsar and pulled out a sheet of paper.

"In view of the fact that your friends are attacking Ekaterinburg to try to save you, and your relatives in Europe continue their assault on Soviet Russia," Yurovsky began reading in a pompous voice, "the presidium of the Ural Regionial Soviet, following the will of the revolution, has decreed you must be shot. . . ."

The tsar blinked. He turned and looked at his family as if hoping they could explain everything.

"What?" the tsar asked numbly. "What?"

The Romanovs and their servants stood frozen in confused terror.

"So then . . . we're not being taken anywhere?" Dr. Botkin asked, still not getting it.

These people, Jonah thought. *They knew their lives were in danger. They knew death was coming for them. But they didn't know it was coming now.*

"I don't understand. Read it again. . . . ," the Tsar mumbled. Was he truly that befuddled? Or was he just bargaining for a little more time?

Yurovsky went back to reading, but Jonah missed the first part of what he said because Daniella hissed at him, "Almost got it—"

Jonah watched her pull threads from her seam. Yurovsky was reading so loudly now that Jonah couldn't tune him out anymore: ". . . has decreed that you, the former tsar, Nicholas Alexandrovich Romanov, must be shot for your crimes against the people. . . ."

Jonah turned and saw the tsarina and Olga cross themselves. He saw Chip and Katherine motioning to him and Gavin and Daniella—urgent gestures that undoubtedly meant, *Get out of there now!* But then Jonah stopped watching, because Daniella shoved a heavy rock into his hand—the diamond.

"Hope you've got a good plan for that," Daniella muttered.

"Me too," Jonah muttered back.

The gem in his hand was large for a diamond—somewhere between a marble and a golf ball. It was undoubtedly worth millions. But Jonah barely glanced at it.

Instead he rolled it out to the tips of his fingers, reared his arm back, and hurled the diamond toward the single lightbulb overhead.

TWENTY-SIX

Baseball had never been Jonah's sport. He'd never been good at accurate throws. But maybe his problem had been that he just needed a diamond to throw with, because this one zinged straight and true toward the ceiling. It smashed perfectly into the single lightbulb, giving off a burst of shattering glass.

The room instantly went dark.

Thanks to the tracer lights, Jonah could still see fairly well, but he knew that the Romanovs and the guards would see only unending blackness around them. The guards were clustered in the doorway now, their weapons ready, but Yurovsky was screaming, "Hold your fire! Hold your fire! Don't shoot me by mistake!"

"Then get out of the way!" one of the guards shouted back.

Jonah saw the tsar swing a fist and punch Yurovsky in the jaw, while Dr. Botkin grabbed the commander and held the man in front of him like a human shield.

"I can't get out of the way! They've got me trapped!" Yurovsky screamed.

But even as he spoke, Yurovsky was reaching into his pocket and slowly pulling his arm back. What was he getting?

Jonah suddenly understood, but he was too far across the room to do anything but warn the others: "He's got a gun! Yurovsky's got his own gun!"

Jonah's shouts seemed to get lost in the other shrieks and screams around him. But then Chip was at Yurovsky's side, yanking the newly revealed gun from the man's hand. Chip wrapped his own hands around the gun and pressed the barrel against Yurovsky's temple.

"Tell your men to stand down!" Chip ordered him. "Tell them to step aside and let the Romanovs leave, or else you're a dead man too!"

Chip, of course, could only say that in English, but Dr. Botkin was thinking clearly enough now to shout the same thing after him in Russian.

Okay! Jonah thought. *This is working even better than I expected!*

He hadn't thought they'd be able to do much more

than yell something like *Everybody run for the stairs!* But now, with Chip taking Yurovsky hostage, this could be orderly and calm. Nobody would get shot even by mistake.

If we're really lucky, we might even end up driving away in that truck, Jonah thought a little giddily.

"Madame Demidova, Mr. Trupp, Mr. Kharitonov, hold on to me, and I'll lead you out of here," Anastasia—no, Daniella—was saying in the darkness. She'd separated completely from her tracer.

Jonah realized that, as a time traveler like him, she would be able to see by the light of the tracers. However, even that light seemed to be growing dimmer and dimmer.

Because so many of the tracers are dead or dying, Jonah thought.

Even the tracer version of Anastasia was lying dim and almost lifeless on the floor where Daniella had left her behind. How horrifying must that be for Daniella to see?

"You take the servants on out right now," Jonah told her, hoping she wouldn't look around. "Katherine and Gavin and I can get everyone else."

But Daniella wasn't making much progress, as the three servants were screaming and crying and praying and maybe hadn't even heard her. Katherine and Gavin were having the same problem with the tsarina and the oldest

Romanov girls. And Dr. Botkin was refusing to let go of Yurovsky and walk away.

That at least makes sense, Jonah thought. *He doesn't know who Chip is and he can't see the gun in Chip's hand—he's just trying to keep control.*

So maybe none of them would get out of the cellar quickly. But it would still work. Chip still had the gun to Yurovsky's head.

Jonah glanced out toward the room where the guards were standing, to find out if they had indeed stepped aside from the doorway. It looked like they had: Jonah couldn't actually see any of them from this angle. But he could see something else: an additional glow that wasn't tracer light, coming from the direction of the stairs.

"Hello?" a thin, reedy voice cried out. "Alexei? Are you down there?"

A boy came into view, carrying a lantern.

It was Leonid Sednev, the kitchen boy.

TWENTY-SEVEN

Bonus! Jonah thought. *Now he'll be able to lead us to the Elucidator and we can make the Romanovs invisible and they really will be safe, long-term.*

But in the next moment Jonah saw one of the guards leap toward Leonid, wrap his arm around Leonid's neck, and point a gun at the boy's head.

"Let Yurovsky go or I shoot!" the guard screamed.

The wails and screams and cries echoed even louder around Jonah. Jonah might have even wailed himself.

How could we have lost the advantage so quickly? he wondered. *There's not even time to translate for Chip. . . .*

But Chip already understood—and was reacting. He tightened his grip on Yurovsky and yelled back, "Let Leonid go or I'll shoot!"

Oh, yeah, Jonah thought. *That's how you negotiate.*

This time it was Gavin repeating Chip's words in Russian: "Let Leonid go or Yurovsky's a dead man!"

The guard holding Leonid looked confused in the dim glow of the lantern light. He took a halting step forward, dragging Leonid with him, bringing the circle of light closer.

"Show yourself," the guard said. "How do I know you're even holding Yurovsky?"

Jonah saw Katherine rush to Chip's side and poke her finger against Yurovsky's chest.

"You tell the guard you're being held," she ordered him. "Tell them you've got a gun at your head!"

Yurovsky just tried to squirm away.

"P-p-please," Leonid stammered. It didn't seem like such a big deal anymore that he was a teenager who already had facial hair. He still sounded terrified out of his wits. "Don't hurt me. I just came to say good-bye. I heard the fighting out in the mountains and I heard the truck and I figured the guards would be taking the Romanovs somewhere else. . . . Look, this proves I'm telling the truth."

He held out a cloth knapsack and said pleadingly, "I just wanted to bring Alexei's toy soldiers back, so he could take them with him. . . ."

The toy soldiers! Jonah thought. *That means he has the Elucidator here! That means we can get it back!*

He took off running toward Leonid. Halfway there, Jonah realized Katherine was sprinting alongside him. They reached Leonid together and knocked the knapsack from his hand.

"Let's divide the pile in half—faster that way," Katherine hissed at Jonah.

Before the knapsack even hit the floor, Jonah was already tugging it open, preparing to shove half the toy soldiers toward Katherine and pull half of them toward himself. In the lantern light this was bound to look strange: the knapsack falling, the toy soldiers seeming to move around by themselves. But Jonah was beyond caring about things like that right now.

Jonah grabbed a handful of toy soldiers and practically threw them at Katherine.

And that was when he heard the first gunshot.

TWENTY-EIGHT

It sounded close.

But any gunfire would sound close in this small, enclosed space, so Jonah still had hope as he glanced up.

It was hard to hold on to that hope as he heard the second, the third, the fourth, and the fifth gunshot. They came so rapidly and in such quick succession that they might as well have been machine-gun fire.

Jonah braced himself for a horrific scene: blood everywhere, the wounded and the dead falling to the floor, just as much chaos and mayhem and screaming as he'd seen (but not heard) when the tracer guards had fired upon the tracer Romanovs.

Jonah still didn't hear any screaming this time, which was odd. In fact, he heard nothing after that fifth gunshot. And at first his eyes couldn't make sense of what he saw:

no chaos, no mayhem, no one falling . . . for that matter, no one moving at all. Olga, Tatiana, and Maria were clustered protectively around their mother, frozen in the motion of holding her up. Gavin and Daniella were flat on the ground, but it looked like they'd dived there to get out of the way of the bullets, not that they'd been hit. Chip, Dr. Botkin, and the tsar were still clinging stubbornly to Yurovsky, but he'd stopped fighting against their grasp.

The guards stood clumped around the doorway between the two rooms. Five of them had their weapons aimed, curls of smoke frozen above the barrels.

It was only when Jonah saw the bullets themselves frozen in midair that he finally understood what had happened.

"Who stopped time?" he asked. "Can the Elucidator do that now? Katherine, did you find the Elucidator and say the command that quickly?"

Katherine squinted up at him—he was relieved to see that she could still move.

So this is just a normal case of stopped time? Jonah wondered. *Where everything's frozen except the people who have traveled through time?*

Though, what was ever "normal" about time travel or frozen time?

"I didn't do anything," Katherine said, sounding as

baffled as she looked. "I don't have the Elucidator." She glanced down at her handfuls of unsorted toy soldiers. "At least, not that I know of."

Someone behind Jonah made a small noise—maybe a whimper. Jonah looked around and realized that the frozen glow of Leonid's lantern had reached the tips of the tsar's boots.

So the guards knew where he was, and that's why they started shooting, Jonah thought.

All five of the bullets suspended in midair had been speeding toward the general vicinity of the tsar. They were various distances away. But—Jonah stood up and looked at the exact angles—only two of them were on course to actually hit him.

One bullet looked like it was about to hit Dr. Botkin.

One bullet seemed about to graze Yurovsky's wrist.

And one bullet was headed straight for Chip's heart.

It was Chip who had whimpered.

"Chip! Get out of the way!" Jonah screamed. "Before time starts again!"

"If I do, the bullet will just hit one of the servants behind me!" Chip protested. A trickle of sweat inched down his face.

"You and your medieval chivalry," Jonah grumbled. He flicked the bullet toward the floor. It bounced. Jonah stepped on it to keep it from hitting anyone else.

Katherine zoomed past him and dived for the other four bullets, knocking them toward the floor as well.

From the direction of the stairs, Jonah heard someone clapping. Somehow it sounded sarcastic—wasn't clapping almost always sarcastic when only one person clapped?

"Bravo, bravo!" a voice cried. "It's always so entertaining to see what you Skidmores will come up with next!"

"It's really a shame we can't let you go on," a second voice agreed. "But we refuse to let you destroy time completely!"

Two men stepped out from the shadows.

"Gary and Hodge?" Jonah asked incredulously.

TWENTY-NINE

Before Jonah could say or do anything else, Gavin leaped up from the floor and began racing toward the two men.

"You lied to me!" he roared.

At practically the same moment, Chip whipped around to point his gun at the two men.

"Drop your Elucidators!" he yelled.

In response, Gary aimed his hand—and probably an Elucidator held within it—directly at Chip. The gun immediately jerked out of Chip's hand and glided across the room toward Gary. Gary calmly tucked it into his pocket.

"You think you can fight Elucidators with a twentieth-century gun?" he taunted.

Almost as quickly, Hodge raised his hand toward Gavin. Gavin instantly froze in the midst of running, both his feet off the ground, his left knee cycled up, his elbows jutting out. But it appeared that he'd only been frozen from the neck down: With his head, he still strained forward, uselessly. And he continued to scream at Gary and Hodge: "What did you do to me?"

"Relax, all of you," Gary said lazily. "Well, I guess Gavin can't relax, really, suspended in midair like that. But be at peace, anyway. We're not going to hurt you. We're saving your lives, remember?"

"Oh, yeah?" Katherine challenged, looking up and over her shoulder from her place sprawled on the floor. "Why should we trust anything the two of you say?"

"Because we didn't let time start back up when your brother would have been responsible for killing you," Hodge said. He aimed his hand toward the wall and a scene began playing back from just a moment earlier: Jonah flicking the bullet toward the floor, the bullet bouncing and spinning. . . . The scene froze at a moment when the bullet was clearly directed toward Katherine.

Jonah shivered.

"See what we mean?" Hodge asked. "If we'd just let time start up then . . . Anybody else feel inclined to rush toward us and be frozen like Gavin? Or have their toys taken away from them, like Chip?"

Nobody moved, but Gavin shouted, "I hate you!"

Hodge shrugged and stepped farther out of the shadows.

Jonah noticed that Hodge looked a lot older than he had the last time Jonah had seen him. His hair was grayer, and his clothing hung on him as if he'd lost an unhealthy amount of weight.

Meanwhile, Gary looked even more muscle-bound than before.

If they've come straight from escaping from time prison, he must have been one of those prisoners who spend all their time lifting weights, Jonah thought, staring at the man's bulging biceps.

Jonah and Katherine and their friends had been no match for Gary's muscles before, back in the time cave. Trying to overpower him seemed even more clearly hopeless now. Especially if Gary and Hodge each had an Elucidator, and Gary was holding Chip's gun.

But do we have a chance to outthink them? Jonah wondered.

"What do you want with us?" Jonah asked quietly. "Why are you doing this?"

Both men turned their attention to Jonah.

"Ah, young Mr. Skidmore," Hodge said. "You *have* matured. Back in the time cave you would have been running for us just as impulsively as Gavin over there."

He gestured toward the frozen Gavin.

Thanks, Jonah thought. *Way to make Gavin hate me.*

"Gavin's just a lot madder at you than I am," Jonah said evenly. "Because this is his family. His life you're messing with."

Hodge raised an eyebrow.

"And this isn't what your life has become?" he asked. "The constant time travel, the constant danger, the constant difficult decisions . . . when all you ever wanted to do was stay in the twenty-first century and stick your head in the sand and pretend none of this has anything to do with you?"

"Would you just answer Jonah's questions and stop trying to distract us?" Katherine demanded.

Gary laughed.

"Sounds like neither of them is as easy to distract as they used to be," he said condescendingly.

"Daniella? Chip?" Hodge called out. "Would either of you like to add your perspective to this discussion?"

Daniella lifted her head slowly from the floor. She gazed around fearfully at the frozen Romanovs and servants and guards, at the mostly frozen Gavin.

"I don't have the slightest idea what's going on," she whispered.

Katherine went to huddle beside Daniella. Jonah heard his sister starting to explain, "See, sometimes time travelers can stop time, but anyone who's traveled through time isn't affected . . . not usually, anyway . . ."

Chip stepped out slightly from behind Yurovsky.

"I think," Chip began, "if your main goal was saving people's lives, you would have done all this very differently. Why did you even want us in 1918?"

"Oh, my dear boy—you think *we* sent you to 1918?" Hodge said mockingly. "Wasn't it Gavin's fault? Or maybe Jonah's? Sometimes it's so hard to pick out cause and effect, event and consequence."

"I didn't want to come here!" Gavin yelled, uselessly jerking his head back and forth. "You promised me I could go to the future! You told me that's what would happen if I typed that code you gave me into an Elucidator!"

"Yes, yes, that is still where you're headed," Hodge said, waving his arm dismissively. "We just didn't tell you there'd be one little detour along the way."

Jonah looked from the calmly mocking Gary and Hodge to Gavin with his bottled-up fury.

"You had to do something to fix 1918, didn't you?" Jonah asked. He was finally putting it all together. "When you kidnapped Alexei and Anastasia the first time around, you were lazy and did it in the afternoon. You grabbed them from Alexei's bedroom and took them down to the garden and time-traveled from there, hours before it was safe to take them away. And that's why we all landed in the wrong place, coming back."

"Maybe," Gary admitted. He looked around at the

Romanovs and their servants and the guards, all frozen in anguish and fury and fear and despair. "Who in their right mind *wouldn't* try to avoid coming here tonight?"

"But your laziness must have created too many problems with time, and so to get away with the kidnapping, you had to send Gavin and Daniella back to finish living out the day," Chip continued for Jonah.

"But why did you have to get Chip and Jonah and me involved?" Katherine asked plaintively from the floor beside Daniella.

"You think Daniella and Gavin could have handled this day all by themselves?" Hodge asked. "Of course, we hated to risk any of our investments, especially so many of you all at once. But—"

He's talking about us like we're just "investments"? Jonah thought furiously. *Just things he can send wherever he wants?*

He clenched his teeth and tried not to let Gary or Hodge see how mad that made him. Fortunately, Hodge was still talking.

"But you know, Daniella's coming into all this cold, without the slightest bit of background in time travel," he said. "And Gavin . . . well, Gavin's got that little anger-management problem. . . ."

"Not after I became Alexei," Gavin protested. "Not once I saw how he coped—"

"And that's why you were trying to attack Hodge and me?" Gary asked.

Gavin glowered at him.

"So what's going to happen now?" Daniella asked.

Don't ask that question, Jonah thought. *Don't get them focused on their next step. Keep them talking, so we have time to figure out a plan. . . .*

"No, wait!" Jonah interrupted. "Time's stopped, anyway, so why don't you explain a few other things? How did you do it? How did you break out of time prison without JB and the other time agents finding out?"

"Trade secrets," Hodge growled.

"Now, now," Gary argued. "The boy's asking us to brag. Don't you think he needs some new heroes?"

"Didn't you just get Gavin to do all your dirty work for you?" Katherine taunted. "Yeah, you guys are some heroes, when you have to trick a poor, sick boy into doing what you want."

"I am not some poor, sick boy!" Gavin screamed.

What's Katherine's problem? Jonah wondered. *Why's she trying to get Gavin even more upset? Shouldn't we be trying to join together as a team against Gary and Hodge?*

Everyone else looked toward Gavin, who was trying to pitch a fit as best he could with his whole body frozen except for his head. But Jonah kept his eyes on his sister.

Do you have the Elucidator? she mouthed in Jonah's direction.

The Elucidator?

Jonah looked blankly at Katherine and shook his head.

Get it! she mouthed. *Hide it!*

Jonah had no prayer of tackling Gary or Hodge and wrestling their fully working Elucidators away from them. So he guessed she meant the dumbed-down "parental controls" Elucidator that Gavin had brought from the twenty-first century. So much had changed in the last few minutes that Jonah had almost forgotten how frantically he and Katherine had been searching for it in the last instant before time froze.

But what good is it now? Jonah wondered. *We're already in 1918, so that command is useless. And invisibility? Even if we turn the Romanovs invisible, Gary and Hodge can still see them. They're the big problem now, not Yurovsky and the guards.*

He hoped Katherine had a plan.

He scanned the two piles of toy soldiers lying before him. A tracer guard walked by just then carrying a dead tracer body—*eww, don't look to see who that used to be*—and in the sudden burst of light, Jonah caught sight of a chipped cap on one of the toy soldiers right beside his knee. Quickly Jonah palmed the soldier and slid it into his pocket. But Gary must have caught a glimpse of the motion out of the corner of his eye, because he turned and peered suspiciously at Jonah.

Okay, if he's suspicious, give him something else to be suspicious about, Jonah thought.

Pretending not to notice Gary's stare, Jonah snatched up one of the ordinary toy soldiers. Hiding it with one hand, he dug a thumbnail against the soldier's cap, hoping the motion would scrape away the paint. Then, pointing the soldier at Gary and Hodge, Jonah cried out, "Make Gary and Hodge invisible! Send them back to time prison!"

Both men instantly went translucent—because of the Elucidator in Jonah's pocket, not the toy soldier in his hand. But of course they didn't go anywhere.

No, scratch that. Gary was suddenly diving toward Jonah, tackling him and pounding him flat against the floor.

THIRTY

Jonah's face smashed into one of the piles of toy soldiers; the other pile seemed to have scattered enough to jab into every other part of his body from his neck down to his ankles.

Okay, okay, so I'll have lots of bruises—just don't let Gary take away the toy-soldier Elucidator from my pocket, he thought.

Gary grabbed Jonah's wrist and twisted it slightly, then yanked away the ordinary toy soldier Jonah held in his hand. Gary tore the soldier in half—*he can do that with just his bare hands?* Jonah marveled. *To solid metal?*—then hurled the two halves of the broken soldier into the opposite corner of the room.

"You're an idiot!" Gary exclaimed, hitting Jonah's face and smashing it that much harder into the toy soldiers he was lying on. "Didn't you remember that Elucidator's worthless? Time's stopped! What does it matter if we're invisible or not?"

"I—I had to try something," Jonah mumbled.

He didn't have to work too hard to fake disappointment— he *was* disappointed that he hadn't thought of some distraction technique that wouldn't have required Gary tackling him.

Gary punched him again. But then he backed away without searching for the actual Elucidator.

Don't act happy, Jonah told himself. *But . . . you can act relieved that Gary didn't kill you.*

Stiffly he sat up. He felt his face, and was surprised to discover that it wasn't covered with open sores and gushing blood. It was very tender, but the skin wasn't broken.

Next Jonah patted his ribs and arms and legs to make sure none of them were broken. They ached too, but all his bones seemed to be intact.

Then, surreptitiously, he patted his pants pocket to make sure the real toy-soldier Elucidator was still there.

It was.

Katherine raced dramatically across the room to his side.

"Are you all right, Jonah?" she cried aloud. "Gary didn't hurt you, did he?"

Just to Jonah she whispered, "Do you have it?"

Jonah nodded, hoping she'd understand which

question he was answering. Surely she wouldn't think he could be all right after Gary's tackle.

Hoping he wasn't carrying the charade too far, he hugged Katherine and whispered back to her, "Do you have a plan?"

"Working on it," Katherine whispered.

"Okay, you two, break it up," Gary said, kicking them apart.

The kick hurt almost as much as being tackled.

All that, and Katherine's just "working" on a plan? Jonah thought bleakly.

Hodge was frowning and shaking his head at Gary, as if something about Gary's actions—or maybe Jonah's—really upset him.

"Enough fooling around," he said. "All you kids, gather around Gavin."

"What will happen if we don't?" Daniella asked.

"Ask Jonah how it felt to have Gary tackle him," Hodge replied. "And remember, we've each got an Elucidator, and Gary's got a gun. You've got nothing."

Except a worthless dumbed-down Elucidator and a sister who's just working on a plan, Jonah thought. *Why didn't I try to steal the gun or Gary's Elucidator when he tackled me?*

Gary flexed his muscles, and Jonah remembered why.

So we have to obey Hodge? Jonah wondered. *Isn't there anything else we can do?*

The only ideas he could think of were nothing but delaying tactics.

"If you're thinking about sending us somewhere else, Gavin and Daniella are going to want the rest of their family to come along," Jonah said as he stood up very, very slowly.

"Oh, yes!" Daniella agreed, scrambling up. "We have to save them!"

"You care that much about the rest of the Romanovs?" Hodge asked, rolling his eyes.

"They're our family!" Gavin argued. "Our real family!"

"We love them!" Daniella cried out. To Jonah's surprise, she was blinking back tears.

"Anyhow, nobody deserves to die this way," Katherine agreed, gesturing toward a tracer body that had been so brutalized Jonah couldn't even tell who it was.

"Maybe the tsar did," Hodge said. "Do you know what life was like for most of his subjects during the twenty-two years of his rule? Do you know how incompetent he was, even as he believed his position was divinely ordained? Do you know how many opportunities he missed, how devastating World War One and the Russian Revolution were for his country—partly because he was such a terrible leader?"

"Move it!" Gary said, shoving Jonah forward. "You all want to find out this kind of info, you can look in the history books when you get where you're going."

So Gary and Hodge were planning to send them somewhere. The future?

Well, fine, we'll just hunt up JB and get him to help us, Jonah thought.

Somehow Jonah suspected that Gary and Hodge might have thought of that possibility. And figured out how to prevent it.

But they don't know we have the dumbed-down Elucidator. Maybe there's something we can figure out with that. . . .

Jonah had delayed as long as he could. He was now standing next to Gavin. So were Chip, Katherine, and Daniella.

"Move Leonid over too," Hodge told Gary.

Gary pulled the lantern out of Leonid's hand and put it on the ground. He shoved Leonid's head down, freeing him from the grasp of the guard who was pointing a gun at the teenager. And then, with the stiff, frozen Leonid under his arm, he walked across the room to set him up again beside Gavin and the other four kids.

"So you *are* rescuing our family and the servants too?" Daniella asked eagerly.

"Nope," Gary said. "Just that one."

He jerked his head toward Leonid.

"But why?" Gavin asked.

Hodge hovered behind them, grinning.

"Let's just say it's thanks to you, Gavin," Hodge explained. "When you gave Leonid the toy soldiers this afternoon, that made him think about his buddy Alexei in a different way. So he was brave enough to sneak back over here tonight, hoping to warn you and your family that the guards were out to kill you."

"He was just returning my toy soldiers!" Gavin protested.

"Don't you think he was smart enough to lie when he saw that the guards already had your family trapped?" Gary asked.

Leonid didn't have much of a plan, Jonah thought. *But neither did the rest of us.*

"Anyhow, that blind, stupid courage and loyalty—it's the kind of quality that makes missing children from history quite valuable on the adoption market of the future," Hodge said.

"You think Leonid is valuable, but not Olga, Tatiana, or Maria?" Daniella asked incredulously. "Or Mama or Papa or . . ."

Hodge glanced toward the cluster of frozen Romanov females.

"How old are your sisters, again?" he asked.

"Olga's twenty-two, Tatiana's twenty-one, and Maria's nineteen," Daniella said.

"That one's borderline, then," Gary said, pointing to Maria. "It didn't seem worth it the last time, but if we're going to have to fake one more death, we might as well fake two."

"Okay, kid," Hodge told Daniella. "We'll compromise. You can have one of your sisters."

"But, but—," Daniella sputtered. "The others—"

It was too late. Gary had already shoved Maria—and only Maria—over beside Daniella. Hodge was already lifting his hand toward them, the glow of his Elucidator shining through his fingers.

"Meet you there!" he cried.

And then Jonah felt himself begin spinning through time with the others.

THIRTY-ONE

Leonid and Maria both instantly unfroze and started screaming.

"What happened? Where are we?" Leonid yelled.

"Are we dead?" Maria asked forlornly. "Did they shoot us all? But—where's the rest of our family?" She squinted at Daniella and Gavin, then at the still-transparent Chip, Katherine, and Jonah beyond. "Alexei, why do you have purple hair? And who are those people? Ghosts? Angels? Why can I see through them?"

Oh, yeah, now that she's traveling through time, she can see other time travelers even if they've turned invisible, Jonah thought.

He wondered what he could do to keep her from going completely hysterical, but Daniella beat him to it.

"Just think of all this as a dream," she advised. "That's how I coped at first."

"You mean, they shot you before the rest of us?" Maria asked. "Oh, Lord, please . . ."

She began reciting a prayer, which seemed to calm both her and Leonid.

Jonah wanted to ask, *Know any good prayers for time travelers who are in big trouble?*

The darkness of Outer Time whirled around them, but somehow the murmured prayer had a calming effect on Jonah, too.

And Gavin seemed positively giddy.

"Hey! I can move again!" he hollered, waving his arms and legs as if to prove it.

"Alexei, you're healed!" Maria cried out. "Everything Mama said about heaven is true—the lame can walk again!" She looked around. "Except we're not really walking, are we? Are we flying?"

Gavin patted his sister on the shoulder and "flew" his way over to talk more quietly with Chip and Jonah and Katherine.

"This isn't so bad," Gavin told the others. "Even if they're sending us to the future, Gary and Hodge will have to deal with the mess in 1918 before they follow us, so—"

"So this is time travel, remember?" Katherine interrupted him. "Gary and Hodge can leave hours or days or even years after us, and still get wherever we're going before us."

"Oh, yeah," Gavin said. He let his arms drop to his side.

"But maybe Gary and Hodge won't expect us to come out fighting," Chip said. "If we arrange ourselves in military formation, we can attack as soon as we arrive, and grab their Elucidators and call JB and get him to help with the Romanovs and—"

"And even if that doesn't work, we'll manage to get in touch with JB *somehow*," Katherine agreed.

"Remember, I do have the dumbed-down Elucidator," Jonah reminded them. "So if we just get away from Gary and Hodge, we can make everyone invisible, not just the three of us, and—"

"I feel funny," Leonid moaned, interrupting the planning. "Small. Do people get smaller in heaven?"

The really odd thing was, his voice squeaked as he said this. Jonah had had problems of his own with that issue, but every other time he'd heard Leonid speak, the older boy's voice had sounded as deep and assured as a man's. The kid had facial hair and everything—what was he doing with a squeaky voice?

"I feel weird too," Daniella agreed. "Shorter. Hey! Stop that! I was short enough to begin with!"

"Jonah?" Katherine said, in her *I'm trying not to freak out, but I really want to* voice. "Remember that tooth I had that took forever to come in after the baby tooth fell out? Now it's shrinking back into my gum. No—now it's gone!"

"What are you talking about?" Jonah asked, and his voice wasn't squeaky. It had changed completely—in the wrong direction. Now his voice sounded as clear and high-pitched and childish as it had two or three years ago.

"Oh, no," Chip moaned. "Oh, no. I know what's happening!"

His voice also sounded childish and as clear as a bell. Jonah hadn't met Chip until right before they'd both turned thirteen—he'd never heard Chip sound so young. He sounded ridiculous.

But Jonah felt no desire to laugh.

"This is why Gary and Hodge weren't worried about us planning any military maneuver or rebelling against them when we get to the future," Chip moaned. "We're getting younger and younger by the minute. We're all going to be babies by the time we land!"

THIRTY-TWO

"Not me!" Gavin argued. "Remember, they promised me, they said I wouldn't have to start over—"

But his voice too came out sounding childish, more suited for a sweet little elementary-school kid than a middle-school tough with dyed hair. Jonah squinted at the other boy: The purple streak appeared to have vanished, and his hair had shrunk to above his ears.

None of us should be changing like this! Jonah thought, trying to keep his own panic at bay. *People don't un-age just because they're traveling through time!*

He'd time-traveled more than a dozen times without changing his age at all.

Except for that one time . . .

Gary and Hodge had changed his age on his first trip through time. When they'd kidnapped all the missing children from history in the first place, the two men had un-aged all of the children back to being babies.

So did they program the Elucidator with the same kind of command this time around? Jonah wondered.

He could feel the panic starting to surge over him, in spite of his best efforts to hold it off.

"What are we going to do?" Katherine wailed. "We get to the future, we won't memember anything."

Did she really just say 'memember'? Jonah wondered. That was one of those little-kid mistakes she used to make all the time. Jonah had seen her once—when? Third grade? Fourth? Fifth?—standing in front of a mirror trying to retrain herself: *Remember, it's "remember." "Remember." The other kids will laugh at you if you say it wrong. Remember . . .*

And Jonah had never heard her say it wrong again.

But now . . .

"Those bad men didn't tell you the truth!" Chip was shouting at Gavin. "They lied about everything! We should beat them up! That's what I want to do!"

Were they all getting younger at the same speed? How much time did they have while they could still think, before they were down to "goo-goo, gaa-gaa" and sucking their thumbs?

Memember, you have a magic toy in your pocket, Jonah told himself. *You can do stuff with it. You can make people invisible. And that's fun in comics and cartoons. But this isn't about fun. This is serious. People could die, so I have to be serious.*

Jonah arranged his face in a very serious expression, so everyone could see that he wasn't trying to have fun. He felt a little hand brush against his and then grab on to his fingers.

"Jo-Jo?" Katherine whispered. "I'm scared. Are you scared too?"

Her blond hair was little-girl wispy now, and her tiny nose was wrinkled up like she was going to cry.

She's really little, Jonah thought. He looked around at the other kids. *She's the littlest one of all.*

Jonah was supposed to take care of her. He was *always* supposed to take care of his little sister. And he got sick of it. But sometimes when she looked up at him like this—like she was so sure he'd be able to fix everything—he kind of liked it. He kind of thought, *Well, maybe I can fix everything.*

"I'm royalty, so I'll get to marry a king or a prince when I grow up," Maria told him, giggling a little. "Are you a king or a prince?"

"I don't think so," Jonah said. He could have told her he was adopted, so there was no telling *what* he was. But his mommy had told him he didn't have to tell people about that unless he felt like it. And right now he didn't feel like it. Because he needed to be serious. He needed to fix everything.

Jonah pulled the toy soldier from his pocket. He looked at the toy soldier and the toy soldier looked back at him.

"What else can you do besides make people invisible?" Jonah asked, because he'd kind of forgotten.

Words glowed above the toy soldier's head:

I CAN:
- TAKE PEOPLE TO 1918
- GRANT INVISIBILITY
- UNDO INVISIBILITY COMMANDS
- LIST MY LIMITED FUNCTIONS

The soldier was a toy—why did it have to use such big words? It took Jonah way too long to puzzle out the words "invisibility" and "commands" and "functions." By the time he looked up again, Katherine was sucking her thumb. Leonid was crying, but trying to hide it. Daniella and Maria were clinging to each other, terrified. Gavin and Chip were fake-punching each other, maybe practicing to fight for real.

We keep going, we're all just going to get smaller and smaller and smaller, Jonah thought. *It's hard to win fights when you're really small.*

"Take us all back," he told the toy soldier in his hand. "To 1918? Is that what it's called?"

Jonah felt like he was in a car where his mommy or daddy hit the brake really hard. His body wanted to keep flying forward. But it couldn't. Instead he went backward.

"We turned around!" he yelled to all the others. "Everything's going to be okay! We're going back!"

Leonid started crying harder.

THIRTY-THREE

They landed on something hard.

Floor, Jonah thought. *Basement . . . in that old house again. Where those kids lived when they were other people. No . . . their prison.*

Jonah couldn't tell if he was still a little kid or if he was just confused from timesickness. He blinked hard, trying to bring his vision back into focus as quickly as possible.

"What the—," somebody said.

Gary and Hodge were standing over them, in the same positions they'd been in when Jonah and the others had vanished from 1918.

"Maybe they're just decoys," Hodge said. "A time agency trick."

"But nobody knows we're here!" Gary protested. "And why would the time agency make them look younger?"

So we're all still . . . little kids? Jonah wondered.

He decided there was a trick to thinking with a time-sick little-kid brain. He could still remember everything that had happened to him as a thirteen-year-old, but he had to make himself really, really brave not to hide from those memories.

Gary and Hodge are bad guys, he thought. *Maybe if I don't move, they'll think I'm just sleeping and they won't do anything.*

"Get that lightbulb back," Hodge said. "Let's make sure before we panic."

Gary turned around, pointing at the light. Then there was a sound like glass shattering—no, un-shattering? The lightbulb glowed overhead once more.

"What is that, twenty-five watts?" Hodge complained.

Gary bent over one of the other kids—Leonid, maybe? Gavin? Jonah couldn't see well enough to tell who it was in the dim light. And he couldn't tell if they were little kids like him. If they were, would they be braver little kids than Jonah?

"Feels like real human skin," Gary reported.

Hodge snorted.

"Yeah, and don't you think there's a chance the time agency has advanced enough to make that realistic too?" he asked.

"Hodge, I am not spending another minute in time

prison," Gary said, sounding panicky now. "If they're onto us, we've got to get out of here!"

"Now, now," Hodge said soothingly. "We covered all our tracks perfectly. Don't be hasty giving up so much treasure." He seemed to be squinting straight down at Jonah. "Remember, that one was holding on to the dumbed-down Elucidator a few moments ago."

"And then I destroyed it and threw it to the other side of the room!" Gary protested.

"We really should remember to pick it up before we go," Hodge muttered, still staring at Jonah. "Unless . . . maybe that wasn't the real Elucidator? Maybe he knew exactly what he was doing?"

Jonah heard a rustling near his head.

"Fight," Chip whispered weakly in his ear. "Got to fight while still . . . can surprise them."

Jonah turned his head and saw that Chip had managed to squeeze his hands into fists.

Chip's brave, Jonah thought. *Chip's thinking like a big kid, even though he's little too.*

Jonah tried to tighten his own fingers into fists as well, but his hands were so numb he couldn't tell if it worked or not.

Anyhow, how can we win a fight against those big, mean men when we're so little? Jonah wondered. *We couldn't beat them before. And they're not surprised anymore that we're here.*

Jonah wanted to curl up into a little ball and hide his face and pretend that Gary and Hodge didn't even exist. But he forced himself to keep thinking about Gary and Hodge, to keep remembering what he'd known about them when he was a big thirteen-year-old.

Is there something else I could surprise them with? Jonah wondered. *Something that would scare them more than little kids' fists?*

"Maybe someone in the group had a second Elucidator we didn't know about," Gary said.

"We would have known," Hodge muttered. "They would have used it to call that goody-goody JB a long time ago. No, I think we have to consider the possibility that this one is smarter than we thought."

He was bending over Jonah now, patting down his sleeves, his chest . . .

He's going to find the Elucidator, Jonah thought. *That nice toy soldier that told me what he could do before . . .*

Jonah didn't have time to ask the toy soldier questions again. He wasn't strong enough to fight with Hodge over the toy soldier. Right now he wasn't even strong enough to lift his hand and push Hodge's hand away, just to buy another minute or two.

Isn't there anything I can tell the toy soldier to do in the next three seconds before Hodge takes it away? Jonah wondered.

It was hard to think with his brain still so fuzzy from

the timesickness—and still so young, no matter how much he tried to fight it—and with Hodge poking at him. And someone had started moaning beside him. Daniella, maybe?

"Save . . . ," she whispered. "Save . . . family . . ."

Jonah couldn't think of anything he could do to save himself or the other kids in the next three seconds. But that word Daniella said, "family," jogged something in his memory. If time started again, Daniella's family would be in great danger once more, especially since Gary and Hodge had turned the light back on. Jonah had been so proud of protecting the Romanovs by throwing that diamond and breaking the lightbulb before. There was no way he would be capable of throwing anything else all the way up to the lightbulb right now. But he could do something else to protect the Romanovs, something he'd known about the last time he was in 1918, before the timesickness, before he got little-kid brain. . . .

Oh, yeah, he thought.

"Make all the Romanovs invisible," Jonah whispered. "And their servants. And their doctor."

He couldn't remember the doctor's name anymore, but maybe it didn't matter.

"What did you just say?" Hodge asked. He stopped patting down Jonah, and whipped his head back to look at the Romanovs lined up in the center of the room. "Oh, no. Oh, no . . ."

He instantly scrambled away from Jonah and grabbed Gary by the arm.

"Restore time after we leave!" Hodge cried. "Restore all the children's ages, too! Restore—"

"Don't worry about any of that!" Gary screamed. "We've got to get out of here! Exit now!"

And then both men vanished.

Jonah could have sworn he blacked out for a few moments. He woke again in such a haze of timesickness that he was sure of only one thing:

The sound of gunfire was back.

THIRTY-FOUR

Jonah had heard Hodge say, *Restore all the children's ages, too!*
But he still felt like reacting like a little kid. He cringed
away from the noise and put his hands over his ears.

"Stop," Jonah whispered. "Stop time again. Stop all of
this."

Time didn't stop, and neither did the gunfire. Now
there were screams and wails and weeping mixed in with
the sounds of all the guns going off. A woman's voice cried,
"Nicky! Where did you go? Niii-cky!"

Rough men's voices screamed, "Is this a trick? Have
they escaped? The light's back, but we can't see them!"

The commander yelled back, "It's just the smoke from
the gunfire blocking your view! They were holding on to
me a second ago! Keep shooting!"

Jonah heard more gunfire.

"You can't do this to my family!" Gavin screamed. "Or my friends!"

Jonah saw Gavin stand up—or, rather, the outline of Gavin, the translucent Gavin who would be invisible to anyone who wasn't a time traveler. And he was a thirteen-year-old again. Gavin weaved his way toward the guards who were now all lined up along the doorway between the two rooms, their guns raised.

"Stop!" Gavin screamed, shoving hard against the barrel of the nearest guard's gun. He pushed it into the gun barrel of the next guard over.

And then a translucent Daniella was right beside Gavin, screaming along with him, "Don't shoot our family!"

Jonah couldn't see what happened next because of all the smoke. He couldn't hear what else they said because all the screams and gunshots blurred together into a single echoing roar in Jonah's ears.

He closed his eyes. Why did he feel so faint all of a sudden?

The noise seemed distant now, almost like a dream. Someone was crying, and Jonah couldn't tell if it was right beside him or barely within earshot.

"Jonah? Jonah? Can you hear me?"

It was Katherine. Of course it was Katherine, who'd always been there by his side in all of their time-travel adventures.

Even if I were dying, she'd probably see it as just another chance to tag along, Jonah thought. He started to chuckle at his own joke but found he couldn't get a sound out of his throat.

And then he didn't feel like laughing anymore.

What does it feel like when you're dying? he wondered. *What if you get shot? Would you even know it, if you were lying on a floor in a little room with gun after gun after gun going off, and you couldn't see anyone in particular shooting at you? Or would you just go all numb and floaty like . . . like I feel right now?*

Am I dying, God? God? God?

Jonah forced himself to open his eyes, because if he was dying, he really wanted to know why.

And what he saw was the worried face of his friend JB staring straight down at him.

THIRTY-FIVE

Dreaming, Jonah thought. *I'm just dreaming, seeing what I want to see.*

He blinked, and when he opened his eyes again, JB was still there.

"Hey, buddy," JB whispered. "We're getting you out of here."

"And the others?" Jonah tried to say. "You're rescuing all of us, aren't you? And Daniella and Gavin's family and friends?"

He couldn't actually tell if any of those words came out, because his mouth felt numb and his ears seemed to have stopped working. He also couldn't tell if JB said anything in reply, or even if JB was trying to say something, because Jonah's vision was blurring into darkness as well.

And then Jonah was waking up in a room filled with

light. He opened his eyes not to a single twenty-five-watt bulb in a dirty basement at two a.m., but to a place where everything gleamed and glowed, clean and bright.

And safe. For the first time since he'd sat down with Katherine at the computer in his own home to look up missing children in history, Jonah actually felt safe. He seemed to be lying in some kind of a hospital bed now, but there were no beeping monitors or rushing medical workers anywhere around. Everything was calm and still.

"Are we in . . . a time hollow now?" Jonah asked. It was a struggle, but he managed to get all the words out, to make his unreliable voice box sound out each syllable.

But it really is my voice again, he thought. *My thirteen-year-old voice, squeaks and all.*

He felt a rush of fondness for his own voice, for being thirteen.

"He's awake!" someone squealed beside him. "He's awake, he's awake, he's awake!"

Katherine, of course. Jonah felt a rush of fondness for her as well, for the way she always stuck by his side, no matter what. At the moment, Jonah didn't even mind that she seemed to want to turn his opening his eyes into a reason to make up a cheerleading chant. Jonah blinked, and her face swam into focus—her almost-twelve-year-old face, so familiar, even with a bruise across the right cheekbone and a tangled strand of blond hair hanging down into her eyes.

We're both the right ages again, Jonah thought in relief. That proved that everything had worked out, didn't it?

Then Jonah remembered that Hodge had wanted all the kids to be their right ages again too.

"I've been thinking and thinking about how we're going to explain my broken arm and all your wounds to Mom and Dad, and . . . ," Katherine began.

Jonah blinked hard, maybe missing some of what she was saying.

"Broken . . . arm?" he said, latching onto the words that seemed the most understandable.

Katherine waved something pink above his face. A cast. A cast encasing her right arm, from her elbow to her wrist.

"It was just the tiniest crack in the bone," she said, "That's why it didn't hurt too bad, except for right after I hit the floor."

She means when the guards pushed us into the cellar, back at the beginning, before we turned invisible, Jonah thought. *So Katherine must have had a broken arm the whole rest of the time we were in 1918, and she didn't say a thing about it after . . . after being in the garden with Chip . . .*

Jonah's brain was so fuzzy. Maybe she'd complained and complained and he just didn't remember it?

Katherine was still talking.

"But the broken arm is no big deal. It's really your bullet wounds we have to worry about—"

"Bullet," Jonah repeated numbly. "Did you say . . . *bullet* wounds? Was . . . was I shot?"

Katherine whirled around to talk to someone just outside Jonah's range of vision.

"JB, he doesn't remember anything!" she complained.

"Yes, I do," Jonah protested, but he probably didn't sound very convincing, because he was also scrunching up his face—*ouch, why does that hurt?*—and trying to figure out what he actually did remember.

Me and Katherine in the cellar . . . And then me and Katherine and all the Romanovs and . . .

Now JB hovered over Jonah.

"Shh, Jonah, you just need to lie still and rest for now. Take it easy," he told him.

Jonah ignored this.

"You came and rescued us," Jonah muttered, still squinting in confusion. "If I have bullet wounds . . . why didn't you come and rescue us *before* I got shot?"

JB sighed. Jonah realized that the man looked just as battered as Katherine, with a streak of dirt across his face and some sort of powdery dust or ash making his brown hair look gray.

"Believe me, I wish I could have," JB said, shaking his head. "But I didn't even know you were in 1918 until you made the entire Romanov family invisible. That set off alerts at time headquarters, and we rushed in to rescue you as soon as we could. But 1918 is a very damaged year, and Gary and Hodge made it worse with their clumsy attempts to cover up their crime. So we couldn't get in for five minutes. Five whole minutes of you lying in that shooting gallery . . ."

Jonah shivered and was a little surprised that this motion didn't hurt.

They've probably numbed me, wherever the bullets actually hit, he thought.

He didn't want to think about bullets being lodged in his own body. He let his brain skip to another question.

"So if we'd just gone wild and crazy and made the Romanovs invisible earlier in the day, you would have rescued us then?" he asked.

"No," JB said solemnly. "If you'd gone wild and crazy and made the Romanovs invisible earlier in the day, that would have altered history so completely that time itself would have collapsed."

"Quit saying things like that!" Katherine complained. "You're just trying to scare us."

She sounded as defiant as ever, but behind the bruises

her face had gone pale. Evidently this was news to her, too.

"Yes," JB said, "I am trying to scare you. Because that *is* what would have happened. And because, no matter how much I've tried to protect you, the two of you keep getting pulled back into the past."

"Hey, it's not our fault!" Jonah said. "Believe me, we didn't ask Gavin to kidnap us! I didn't get up this morning—I mean, the last morning I spent in the twenty-first century—and think, 'Okay, I feel like getting shot today! How about I go back to 1918 and see what it feels like to hang out around a bunch of trigger-happy Russians?'"

"It's like you're blaming us for not being able to fight our own fate," Katherine protested.

Jonah was surprised that she had used that word "fate." Was Katherine thinking about destiny and free choice every bit as much as he was?

"I'm not blaming you," JB said in an even tone. "I'm blaming Gary and Hodge for putting their own greed ahead of everything else. I'm blaming them for being so eager to escape time prison and continue their nefarious business that they put the fate of the entire space-time continuum in the hands of thirteen-year-olds."

"I'm only eleven," Katherine muttered, which was another surprise, because normally she would have happily accepted credit for being older than she actually was.

"That is, when I'm not even younger. . . . How far back did I go when we un-aged going through time? Was I five? Six?"

"Is that supposed to make me feel better?" JB asked despairingly. "The thought of a five- or six-year-old changing the world?"

Jonah started trying to sit up, but decided that that would put him at too much risk for fainting. And that wouldn't help him make his point.

"But everything turned out okay, right?" he asked. "Sure, we were little kids for a while, but we're the right ages now. And maybe I have a few bullet wounds, but obviously they're not *that* bad, are they?"

He hoped JB and Katherine couldn't tell that he felt like fainting just at the thought of bullet wounds. He forced himself to go on.

"And you've probably got me in quarantine or something and Katherine was the only one you let in because she wouldn't shut up about it, but everyone else is okay, aren't they?" he asked. "Chip and Daniella and Gavin and . . ."

His voice faltered, because JB was staring back at him with such an odd expression on his face.

"Aren't they okay?" Jonah repeated.

"You and Katherine will be fine," JB said. "*Are* fine, I mean, though as Katherine pointed out, we're going to have to handle the issue of explaining your bullet wounds to your parents very, very carefully. But the others . . ."

"You told me you were taking care of them!" Katherine shrieked. "You told me not to focus on anyone but Jonah for right now. Aren't they okay? Chip? Isn't Chip okay? Where is he?"

She grabbed JB's shirt, and at first Jonah thought she was actually going to try to start hitting him until he told her about Chip. But she was actually reaching into JB's shirt pocket, as if desperate to find his Elucidator.

"Take us to Chip!" she cried. "Let us see for ourselves—"

JB pulled back.

"I promise, I'll tell you exactly what's going on," he said. "But you can't do anything rash. I have my Elucidator set on triple security codes, so don't think for a minute that you can grab it away from me and do whatever you want."

"Tell!" Katherine exploded.

JB pursed his lips grimly.

"Chip . . . ," he began slowly. "Chip and the others are still back in 1918. Some things are still up in the air, but . . . I have to prepare you for the possibility that—"

"That what?" Jonah asked, just as impatient as his sister.

JB looked down, his voice barely a whisper.

"It may turn out that you two were the only ones we could rescue."

THIRTY-SIX

"What? You left everyone else behind? That isn't even Chip's native time!" Katherine wailed. "Go back and get him! And Gavin and Daniella and—"

"It's not that simple," JB said miserably.

Katherine gaped at him.

"But you're just sitting here doing nothing?" she asked. She'd stopped trying to search for JB's Elucidator, but now she began reaching toward Jonah instead. "Where's the dumbed-down Elucidator, then? Hand it to me, Jonah, and I'll go back and rescue everyone."

"That Elucidator will only take you on a one-way trip, remember?" JB reminded her. "Besides, the 'dumbed-down' Elucidator, as you call it, was taken away as evidence. Stop trying to manhandle Jonah."

Katherine dropped her hands to her side.

"You're not even trying," she moaned.

"Yes, we are," JB said quietly. "The entire agency called an emergency session of our top officials. They'll consider every possibility and—"

"They called a meeting?" Jonah repeated in disbelief. "Chip and the others are in a tiny room with bullets flying everywhere, and all your agency did was call a meeting? Why didn't you just grab them when you grabbed me and Katherine?"

JB closed his eyes momentarily and drew in a deep breath, as if trying to gather the strength to answer Jonah's question. He exhaled and stared back at Jonah.

"We had thirty seconds," JB said. "Just thirty seconds to get in and get out, because all the time around that moment was already so damaged. Gary and Hodge really messed things up, flipping you in and out of time so quickly to readjust your ages, to try to hide what they'd done."

"Is *that* what happened during the time I blacked out?" Jonah asked.

"You *all* blacked out, temporarily," JB said grimly. "Not the safest way to travel through time. And not the safest way to arrive back in the middle of a massacre. . . ."

He looked like he could hardly bear to talk about it.

"And anyhow, how much do you know about 1918?" he asked. "The whole world was changing then—you had all the fallout from World War One and the Russian Revolution, the Spanish flu epidemic . . . Did you know that July 17, 1918, was also the day the *Carpathia* was torpedoed and sank?"

Jonah had never heard of the *Carpathia*.

"But in thirty seconds—," he began.

"In thirty seconds I had just enough time to grab you and Katherine and get out," JB said. "We knew you'd been shot, so we had to get you. I was just lucky that Katherine was right beside you, so I could grab her, too. I only have two hands."

Jonah didn't want to think about how much worse he'd feel if Katherine had been left behind too.

"So why didn't six or seven other time agents go in with you so there'd be twelve or fourteen more hands? Why didn't you send enough people to save everyone?" Katherine argued.

JB sighed.

"That would have caused so much additional damage that none of us would have escaped," JB said. "There were some in the agency who didn't even think it was safe for me to go. I'm, uh, probably facing a reprimand as it is, for not waiting to follow proper protocol before going in."

"But waiting, having a meeting, when there are bullets flying—" Jonah was so angry he couldn't get the words out.

"The meeting's not happening in the same time frame as the flying bullets, remember?" JB said. "Look, does this make you feel any better?"

He pulled out his Elucidator, which looked like the great-great-great-grandson of the most up-to-date iPhone Jonah had ever seen. JB seemed to be typing in password after password, and then he projected an image onto the wall. It showed the cellar room JB had rescued Jonah and Katherine from, evidently only a split second after they'd all left. Amid the clouds of smoke from all the gunfire, Jonah could barely make out the crystalline figures of his friends and the others. Probably the Elucidator's viewpoint was enhanced somehow, and he would be able to see nothing but smoke if he were actually back in the room. But he could tell that Leonid and Maria had baffled expressions on their faces, gazing down at the floor where Jonah and Katherine had been lying. Gavin and Daniella were still standing by the lineup of guards in the doorway, trying to get them to stop shooting. Chip had apparently just stood up, seemingly ready to go help Gavin and Daniella.

Beyond them, the room was in chaos. The tsar was slumped to the floor and Dr. Botkin was bent over him, maybe trying to shield him from the guards' guns. The tsarina was screaming and reaching toward the tsar, but it looked like she had already been hit too. Olga and Tatiana were clustered beside her, motionless with horror and shock. Behind them the maid, the footman, and the cook were equally motionless, but it looked like they had all been writhing on the floor in agony only a moment earlier.

Motionless . . . , Jonah thought.

"You froze time again?" he asked JB.

"No," JB said, shaking his head. "That would have damaged time too. I'm just showing you the next moment after we left that isn't damaged time. Technically speaking, from our perspective, that's the first moment that wouldn't be off-limits to change."

"So change it!" Katherine insisted.

JB ignored her and typed in another command on his Elucidator. A second image appeared on the wall beside the first. This was like watching video rather than looking at a photograph: It was some kind of assembly or legislative body, deliberating in a huge meeting room.

The UN, maybe, Jonah thought, because there were people with all different skin colors and a variety of different clothing.

Then he noticed that everyone in that room was staring toward and pointing at and talking about a huge image on their wall: the same image of the cellar room that JB had called up for Jonah and Katherine to see.

"They're meeting in a time hollow," JB said. "They

could talk for days or months or years about what to do in 1918, and meanwhile not another instant would pass in that cellar room. So there is time for them to consider every possibility, every ramification. They're not, I don't know, sipping coffee and eating doughnuts and waiting for a colleague to second their motions, while back in the cellar someone else is dying with each minute that goes by."

Looking at the two scenes—one moving forward, one still and stopped and waiting—Jonah understood what JB was trying to say. But somehow it didn't make him feel any better. Some of the delegates in the conference room did indeed seem to be sipping coffee and eating doughnuts— or at least some futuristic version of doughnuts that looked like they might have been made out of bean sprouts.

Okay, so I get it that they have all the time in the world to eat and drink and talk and talk and talk and try to come to the best decision, Jonah thought. *But how can they when they're watching all those people in front of them on the verge of death? How can they stand not acting instantly?*

Katherine pointed toward the image of the huge meeting.

"That's where all the decisions are being made?" she asked. "That's where they're meeting right now?"

JB nodded.

"To the extent that anything can be said to happen 'right now' in a time hollow . . . ," he began.

Katherine waved away that distinction.

"Then take us there," she said. "Let us talk to them."

"Yeah!" Jonah agreed.

JB looked closely at both of them, narrowing his eyes, clearly thinking hard.

"All right," he finally said. "Fine."

The bright, artificial room around them disappeared.

THIRTY-SEVEN

In the next moment Jonah felt such an intense burst of pain he couldn't resist screaming.

"Sorry, Jonah, forgot to warn you that coming out of that time hollow you'd get hit with all the pain from your injuries," JB said, patting Jonah's back. "But we'll be in the other time hollow in nothing flat. . . ."

And then they were, and Jonah felt much better.

The three of them landed in the back of the huge assembly room, in chairs that might as well have been pulled out from the table and arranged just for them.

Spectators' seats, Jonah thought. *Just for watching.*

But almost as soon as they landed, JB was already standing up and addressing the crowd.

"The children," he said, "would like to speak."

Um, now, you mean? Jonah thought. *If everyone else gets all the time in the world to think and talk and everything, shouldn't we get a few moments to figure out what we actually want to say?*

Katherine didn't seem to need that.

"Thanks," she said, bouncing up out of her chair.

She walked toward the front of the room so she was positioned right in front of the image of the cellar. She pointed up at it.

"How can you not want to help those people?" she asked. She started gesturing at each individual person. "That's Chip Winston right there, who survived the 1480s and is only in 1918 because he was kidnapped a second time. It wouldn't be fair to him to just let him die there!" She moved her hand slightly to the right. "That's Daniella McCarthy, who was originally Anastasia Romanov—"

"*Romanova*," a snooty-looking woman in the front row corrected her. "With Russian names at that point in time, when it's a female, you add an *a* at the end."

"Okay, sorry. Whatever," Katherine said, rolling her eyes. "That doesn't matter that much right now, does it? What I started to say was, Daniella didn't even know about her original identity until she was in 1918. But wow, was she brave! Doesn't she deserve a chance to live out the rest of her life in the twenty-first century? Doesn't her adoptive family deserve a chance to get her back? And—"

"Little girl," someone interrupted in an annoyed tone.

It was a bearded man standing to the side. "You're wasting our time. We're the experts. I'll warrant that every single one of us in this room already knows more about the people in the Ipatiev House at that moment than you ever will."

Ipatiev House? Jonah thought. *Is that the actual name of the house where the Romanovs were staying? Is beard guy just calling it that to make Katherine and me feel ignorant?*

"And, sure," the bearded man continued, "in an ideal world, if everything were sunbeams and rainbows and butterflies, of course we'd save everyone we could. The past would be completely empty, because how could we bear to keep anyone from enjoying the best life they could possibly have?"

"But—," Katherine began.

The bearded man cut her off.

"This is *reality*," he said. "Every action has *consequences*. Let me just show you . . . oh, I don't know. How about scenario three thousand four hundred eighty-two? Roll it, Humphrey."

Whoever was controlling the image at the front of the room—Humphrey?—must have followed the order, because suddenly the word "simulation" appeared across the image, and the action began to move forward. A shadowy figure appeared next to Gavin and Daniella and clasped a hand over each of their mouths. Then the figure and both kids vanished.

"Looked fine to me," Katherine said.

"Of course," the bearded man said sarcastically. "Now zoom in and slo-mo it."

The scene replayed, but this time the view was changed so that the focus was on Gavin's right elbow. Right when the shadowy figure put his hand over Gavin's face, Gavin's elbow jolted out, knocking the barrel of the nearest gun sideways. In excruciatingly slow motion, the gun went off, sending a bullet up and then into the neck of a nearby guard. The image froze on that guard's anguished face.

"So," the bearded man said, "we kill this man in 1918— and, believe me, that *is* a fatal wound—and this is what happens during the Cuban Missile Crisis in 1963."

Jonah saw a quick flash of people dying: soldiers, men in suits, women in silly-looking netted hats, children sitting at school desks, hunched over books about kids named Dick, Jane, and Sally. Hundreds of people died before Jonah's eyes—no, thousands. Millions.

The word "simulation" stamped across all those deaths didn't exactly make Jonah feel any better.

"That's only one scenario," Katherine said, and Jonah could tell that she was trying to hide the tremble in her voice. "One out of—what was that number? Three thousand something? I bet, from that many possibilities, there's got to be at least one or two where nothing bad happens."

"The problem is, in the original setup, you just can't tell for sure what is going to lead to disaster and what is going to be fine," a kinder-looking man explained from the opposite side of the room. "Things were so dicey in 1918 that everything's a huge risk. We'd have to have a very experienced time agent on the ground, guiding the events. We've run the projections thousands of ways, and there's just too much of a disruption, because of the time it would take any of us to get Chip and the others to see us and trust us and leave with us. . . ."

"Then what if you just send Jonah and me back?" Katherine asked.

"What? You think *children* can fix this problem?" the bearded, sarcastic man exploded.

Jonah heard others gasping and exclaiming, but the noise seemed to come from far away. He was mostly just aware of his own heart, pounding dangerously hard. He had to press his hand against his head just to keep himself sitting up.

Hope nobody's looking at me, he thought. *Hope they're all just listening to Katherine.*

She was still arguing. Jonah forced himself to focus on her words.

"Chip and Daniella and Gavin already trust us," she was saying. "And Leonid and Maria at least met us already, and they could tell the rest of the Romanovs—"

"You want to see what happens if we send you and your brother?" This was the bearded man again. He seemed to have dialed up his sarcasm to its highest level. "Fine. Go sit down and we'll set up the projection."

Jonah hoped that he was the only one who could see that Katherine was shaking as she returned to the chair between Jonah and JB.

Or maybe the problem was that Jonah's vision was still a little messed up?

"Katherine," he whispered to his sister. "I'm not sure that I—"

"Shh. It's starting," Katherine whispered back.

This time the simulation in front of them showed Jonah and Katherine suddenly appearing beside Gavin and Daniella. The Jonah figure collapsed to the floor as soon as he landed, and a pool of red blood circled his body. The Katherine figure turned and began screaming. Just at that sound—even though Jonah and Katherine were invisible, even though they were hidden in the smoke anyway— the guards pointed their guns in their direction and began shooting.

The image froze and faded into black.

"Surely you don't want to see more," the bearded man said.

"Maybe you should show us a projection where you don't put me in the path of a bullet in the first second," Jonah said angrily.

He felt dizzy and sick to his stomach. It really wouldn't help his argument if he fainted or threw up right now.

"My dear boy," the bearded man said, as if he were talking down to a toddler. "We stopped that *before* any bullets struck you. All that blood? That's just from the injuries you already have, reopened by the strain of time travel."

The injuries I already have are that bad? Jonah thought. And then he couldn't focus on anything anymore, because he was too busy telling himself, *Don't vomit. Don't faint. Please, don't let them see how awful I feel. . . .*

"Then wait until Jonah heals," Katherine argued.

"He can't heal as long as he's in this time hollow," the bearded man answered. "He'd have to go back into regular time for that. And none of us can leave this time hollow until we have a decision."

Jonah was ashamed of the relief that flowed through him. But Katherine scraped back her chair and stood up and kept arguing.

"All right then," she said. "Show what happens if you send me all by myself."

Jonah peered at his sister in dismay.

No, no . . . That wouldn't be safe. . . .

He tried to catch Katherine's eye, to get her to understand without him having to say anything. But she had her chin held high and all her attention focused on staring defiantly at the bearded man.

"Very well," the bearded man said. "Humphrey?"

He looked up, possibly toward someone at a control panel at the back of the room. Jonah turned around just in time to see a young woman shaking her head at the bearded man.

"No—you know what? Forget that," the bearded man said. "That would just be ridiculous. Young lady, of course we appreciate your concern, but truly, you must leave this matter to the grown-ups. I don't even know why JB brought the two of you here."

Jonah noticed that all the grown-ups in the room, including JB, instantly dug into their pockets and pulled out Elucidators. Even as the life-size frozen image of the 1918 cellar reappeared at the front of the room, all the grown-ups peered intently down at their miniature screens. JB seemed to have to poke at his Elucidator a little longer than the others—*turning off the triple security coding?* Jonah wondered. JB didn't seem to have time to turn the security back on, because mere seconds later he and all the other adults were looking back up, their expressions a mixture of thoughtfulness and worry and . . .

Hope? Jonah thought. *Is there any reason why any of them should be feeling hope right now?*

What was going on?

"My apologies," JB said, standing up to address the bearded man. "Of course there's no reason to run a projection with just Katherine going. It'd be too dangerous. She'd have to carry a modern, fully functioning Elucidator, and in such a dicey situation, that's directly prohibited by about fifty different regulations. And she'd have to leave it on voice-command mode—again, totally forbidden under the circumstances. And she'd have to get in and out in the thirty seconds before damaged time resumes. And of course she'd have to be prepared for the possibility that her presence would short out some of our controls, and the likely result would be that all the Romanovs would become visible once more. . . ."

"I'm glad you're actually being sensible for once," the bearded man said.

Jonah turned to glare at JB—what a traitor! Jonah didn't want Katherine going back to 1918 by herself either, but he hated how all the time agents acted like he and Katherine were incompetent just because they were kids.

JB wasn't looking toward Jonah, so the glare was

pointless. JB seemed to be concentrating very hard on taking his seat again, aligning the legs of the chair very precisely with the table in front of him. Evidently this was a harder process than JB had expected, because he moved the chair, gave a frustrated sigh, and then put his Elucidator down on the table so he could use both hands to pull the chair into place.

As soon as JB let go of the Elucidator, Katherine snatched it up.

"Voice commands!" she screamed. "Take me back to 1918! Take me there!"

She pointed to the frozen image at the front of the room.

A split second later Katherine was gone.

THIRTY-EIGHT

Instantly Katherine reappeared in the scene at the front of the room.

"No!" Jonah screamed.

He frantically looked around, desperate to find somebody else's Elucidator so he could go rescue his sister. But the nearest Elucidator had just disappeared into an old man's pocket three seats away.

In his current condition, it would take Jonah more than thirty seconds just to get over to that old man.

He whipped his head back to the scene at the front of the room.

As far as Jonah could tell, no bullets had hit Katherine yet.

"If you want to live, grab on to me!" Katherine screamed.

Then she dived down to the floor, flattening her body

against the wood planks. Chip and Leonid hit the floor beside her, each of them clutching Katherine's shirt. It took Jonah a moment to realize that Chip had pulled Daniella along with him, and that Leonid had a grip on Maria's hand.

Numbers appeared at the bottom of the projected scene: a countdown.

18 . . .

17 . . .

16 . . .

"Don't wait too long!" Jonah screamed at the screen before him, as though Katherine could actually hear him. "Get the others and go!"

Gavin, who was still over by all the guards, had whirled around at the sound of Katherine's voice. But he hesitated.

"Mama!" he screamed. "Papa! Olga! Tatiana! Come with us!"

Daniella and Maria were yelling the same things. But either the other Romanovs failed to hear the three teenagers, or they were too terrified and confused—or already too close to death—to respond. Nobody stepped out of the smoke. But their forms seemed strangely solid in the midst of all the smoke.

All the Romanovs and their servants lost their invisibility, just like JB predicted, Jonah realized, a jolt of terror striking his heart.

His terror magnified: Chip and Katherine were fully visible too.

But—the smoke, Jonah told himself. *Surely the smoke will still hide them from the guards. And they won't be there long. . . .*

"Gavin, hurry!" Katherine screamed. "We only have ten seconds!"

No, nine, Jonah thought.

8 . . .

7 . . .

6 . . .

"Katherine, get out of there!" Jonah yelled.

All the dignified grown-ups around him were yelling too.

Gavin stood frozen on the screen, so still that Jonah wondered if time had stopped again. His face was a study in agony and indecision. Then he turned his head and saw the guards.

Four of them, at the sound of Katherine's voice, had pointed their guns in her direction. Whether they could see her through the smoke or not, all four of them were pulling their triggers.

"No! Don't shoot her!" Gavin screamed.

He threw himself in front of the guns.

He landed on the floor, sprawled between the guards and the other kids. Jonah couldn't tell if Gavin had fallen because he'd been shot or if that was just the natural end to his dive.

Of course he was shot, Jonah told himself. *He was standing in front of four guns, and all four of them were going off.*

The countdown on the screen continued.

3 . . .

2 . . .

1 . . .

Leonid laid his hand comfortingly on Gavin's shoulder.

And then the whole pile of downed children vanished from the screen.

They reappeared almost instantaneously in a heap at the front of the room.

THIRTY-NINE

Maria and Leonid were the first to sit up and pull away. They were completely disheveled, their clothing torn, their faces dirty, their hair sticking out at odd angles. But except for a few random cuts and scrapes, they didn't seem to be injured.

They stared around in awe and confusion, their jaws dropped, their eyes wide with wonder.

The bearded man stood behind them and patted their shoulders.

"You're safe now," he assured them. "No one will shoot you here."

Daniella scrambled up beside them. One sleeve of her dress hung in tatters from her shoulder, and she had a smear of dirt or ash on her face that ran from her forehead down to her jaw. But she also looked like she hadn't been hurt.

Physically, anyway.

As soon as she stood up, she began looking around and screaming, "Papa? Mama? Tatiana? Olga?"

She evidently caught a glimpse of the wall behind her, still playing out the scene from the cellar room in 1918. It was hard to see past the haze of dying smoke, but it appeared that the guards had stopped shooting and shooting and shooting.

Now they were moving in with bayonets.

Like before, Jonah thought in horror. *Like what we saw playing out with tracers. When the tracer guards made sure that all the tracer Romanovs and their tracer servants were really and truly dead. Only this time we're watching it happen for real.*

Jonah couldn't be sure how much Daniella had seen or understood of the tracers' movements before. Maybe she'd understood only what would have happened to Anastasia.

But she clearly understood everything she was seeing now.

"No!" she screamed. "No! Not my family! Save them! I've got to go back for the rest of them!"

She looked frantically around, her eyes lighting on Katherine, who was still lying on the floor. She dived toward Katherine, screaming, "Give me that Elucidator! Does this one look like a toy soldier too? Take me back! Take us all back!"

Is it still on voice commands? Jonah wondered. *If she touches it, if she even grabs ahold of Katherine while she's saying stuff like that . . . what will happen? Is she going to take Katherine and everyone else back into danger?*

As quickly as he could, Jonah shoved his chair back and tried to rush toward the front of the room, toward Katherine and Daniella. But "quickly" for him was now an old man's pace. Just lifting his feet was like trying to raise weights tied to his legs.

Before he'd gone two steps, Jonah saw that the bearded man had already grabbed Daniella and was jerking her back from Katherine.

"Are you crazy?" he asked. "That's pointless. It'll only get you killed with the rest of them. There's nothing you can do."

Daniella turned and tried to shove him away. He held on even more tightly, pulling her close.

"Why can't we save them?" she wailed into his chest. "Why? Why do they have to die?" She lifted her head, a gleam of hope in her teary eyes. "I know! We'll go back and try from the beginning, all over again! Send us back a second time, starting in the afternoon, and this time we'll work it all out, we'll save everyone, we'll bring them *all* here. . . ."

Jonah expected the bearded man to start lecturing

her, to unleash the sarcasm he'd used so scathingly on Katherine.

Instead the man hugged Daniella and gently patted her on the head.

"Oh, my dear child," he said. "I'm so sorry. It just doesn't work that way. Not in the real world. You just got the closest thing anyone can have to a second chance, without endangering the rest of humanity. You're still alive. Your brother's alive. One of your sisters is alive. I'm so sorry about everyone else."

Daniella collapsed and kept sobbing.

By now Jonah had reached the front of the room. Someone had had the sense to stop showing the continuing scene from 1918 on the wall. It had been replaced by a column of words:

REST IN PEACE
Nicholas Romanov
Alexandra Romanova
Olga Romanova
Tatiana Romanova
Evgeny Sergeevich Botkin
Anna Demidova
Alexei Trupp
Ivan Kharitonov

Jonah couldn't stand to look at those names.

The ones we failed, he thought. *Maybe if I had been able to go back with Katherine . . . If I hadn't been shot . . .*

He wanted to see Katherine for himself, to make sure that she wasn't hurt. Why wasn't she popping up as quickly as Daniella had?

She was still on the floor beside Chip. She had her hand stretched out, touching Chip's face.

"And see? This time I saved you," she was murmuring.

"Thank you," Chip whispered back.

Oh, no, Jonah. Ugh, ugh, ugh.

It looked like the two of them were about to kiss.

Jonah did not need to watch his little sister kissing his best friend.

Maybe that should make him my former best friend? he wondered disgustedly.

Jonah didn't want to see or think about any of it, especially when he already felt so woozy and nauseated.

Besides, someone was tugging on the right leg of his jeans.

Jonah looked down and saw Gavin on the floor below him.

"Please," Gavin moaned.

Weakly, he motioned for Jonah to bend down beside him. On unsteady legs, Jonah crouched down.

"Please, I'm . . . I'm bleeding to death," Gavin said.

Jonah looked up, a motion that made the room spin. But he managed to scream: "Help! Gavin needs a doctor! Quick!"

Now others were bending down alongside Jonah, by Gavin's side. Jonah started to scoot back out of the way to make room for someone who would know more than just basic first aid. But Gavin clamped his hand on Jonah's arm. He had a surprisingly strong grip. And, just as surprisingly, none of the grown-ups were shoving Jonah away.

"I'm going to die, and there's nothing anyone can do to save me," Gavin said. His face was frighteningly pale, as if most of the blood in his body had already drained away. "So you have to listen to my last words and tell my family. My other family, I mean, my parents who raised me. I'm squared away with the Romanovs. But tell Mom and Dad I'm sorry. I'm not mad at Mom anymore for trying to protect me all the time. I love them and—"

"Young man," a voice said from behind Jonah. "You are in no danger whatsoever of bleeding to death."

"Yes, I am!" Gavin hissed through gritted teeth. He almost sounded angry that anyone could doubt him. "Don't you know I have hemophilia? I have an internal bleed going in my hip that started back in 1918—if you just touch it, you'll feel how warm it is, how much blood is there. And I just got shot three—no"—he looked down at himself—"four times. I'm dying! Quit making me spend my last moments fighting with you! I have important things to say!"

"Yes, you do." This was JB's voice. "And we're going to make sure you have time to say them all. You're not dying. No one has ever died in a time hollow. You're not even getting much blood on the carpet."

Gavin's head lolled forward. Jonah followed his gaze. There was, indeed, no pool of blood forming around Gavin, and no one seemed to be in any rush to treat him.

"How can this be?" Gavin asked, sounding stunned.

"Things don't change in a time hollow," JB explained patiently. "You can't lose any more blood. Of course, you also can't heal, so after we operate and get the bullets out, like we did for Jonah, we'll have to take you somewhere else. But Gavin, I can assure you—you're going to *live*."

Gavin seemed to be struggling very hard to accept this.

"Why?" he finally asked. "How can I deserve that? Why would you help me? After I forced the other kids to go back to 1918, after I put their lives in danger . . . after I sided with Gary and Hodge . . ."

"You get another chance," JB said. "How about if you

help us catch Gary and Hodge and we call it even?"

Gavin's eyes glowed. Maybe it was Jonah's imagination, but it even seemed like some of the color came back to his cheeks.

"Deal," he said.

EPILOGUE

Jonah struggled out of his hospital bed and picked up a basketball lying on the floor. Standing unsteadily—and swaying slightly—he began bouncing the ball up and down. He started to bend a little, dribbling lower and lower.

That's progress, he told himself. *Yesterday that probably would have popped a stitch or two.*

He heard a sigh from the next bed over.

"If you're going to bounce that thing anyway," Gavin said resignedly, "you might as well bounce it back and forth with me."

"Okay," Jonah said, dribbling the ball gradually toward the end of the beds, where there was more space. "I mean, as long as you're sure you won't get hurt."

Gavin made a face at Jonah, then slid out of his own bed and walked toward the open area.

"You know, I'm tougher than you are," Gavin said. "I survived being hit by four bullets. You only took two."

"Oh, yeah?" Jonah retorted. "If you'd wanted, you could have taken my two bullets along with your own. Wouldn't have bothered me."

"What, you really wanted me to die?" Gavin asked.

"Not *then*," Jonah said.

That came out sounding completely wrong. Jonah had been trying for the same kind of jokey tough-guy talk that kids did all the time at school. But somehow it was different when death had been so close for both of them.

Jonah stopped the ball.

"I didn't mean that," he said. "Really, Gavin, there wasn't ever a time that I wanted you dead. You know that, don't you?"

"Would you just shut up and bounce the ball?" Gavin asked roughly.

Jonah gave the ball a gentle toss. Gavin swatted it back to him. They kept going, back and forth and back and forth, in silence.

Jonah and Gavin had been in this hospital room for two weeks, waiting for their wounds to heal enough that nobody would notice anything out of the ordinary when they returned home. Technically, Jonah knew, they were living in the future—the distant future, so far beyond the early twenty-first century that it was long after any moment they'd reach even as very, very old men. But they'd been absolutely forbidden to see any of the actual future. Their room was a perfect replica of a twenty-first-century hospital room, and guards stationed outside their room monitored everyone and everything going in or out.

At one time, such a setup would have driven Jonah crazy with curiosity.

But for now he was fine with sitting in a hospital room that looked like any hospital room back in twenty-first-century Ohio. He was fine with doing nothing more exciting than bouncing a ball back and forth with Gavin.

"Do you actually *care* about basketball?" Gavin asked, finally breaking the silence. "You're trying out for your school team, right? Is that, like, *important* to you?"

Jonah bounced the ball back and forth twice, considering this.

"I don't *care* care," Jonah said. "I think I can make the team—I mean, after I heal. And that would be nice, but it's not that big a deal. It's just for fun. You win a basketball game, great. You lose, so what?"

"It's not life or death," Gavin said.

"Yeah," Jonah agreed. He was surprised that Gavin understood so well. "Yeah, I think maybe that's why I like it."

The laptop computer sitting on Jonah's bedside table began to ring.

"Two o'clock Skype call, right on schedule," Gavin said. "Dude, the others must really miss us."

It wasn't really Skype they were using to talk back and forth with Chip, Katherine, Daniella, Maria, and Leonid in another room. But it was set up to look that way. To Jonah's surprise, even after Katherine's arm had healed, JB still kept all the other kids together in a time-hollow room while Jonah and Gavin were recuperating.

Katherine was the one who'd figured out why.

"Duh, Jonah," she'd whispered during one of their daily calls. "You and Gavin still need to heal medically, but all of us need to heal psychologically. We saw eight people gunned down in cold blood. We actually kind of saw it twice, if you count the first time with the tracers. We've probably all got—what's that thing called? PTSD?"

Jonah could have pointed out that he and Katherine had seen plenty of awful things in other centuries and then just gone back to their normal lives.

But Katherine knew that too.

"I think . . . I think all the time agents are learning from their mistakes," Katherine had continued. "Doesn't it seem like they're doing things differently now?"

Jonah was still thinking about that one.

Gavin had gone to answer the Skype call.

"Really?" he was saying. "Really? That's great!"

"What are you talking about?" Jonah asked, dropping the basketball to go join Gavin with the call.

"Daniella says JB figured everything out about what to do with Maria and Leonid," Gavin told him. "They'll be in the twenty-first century with us. They're going to live with your friend Angela. Leonid's already set to enroll in high school, and Maria's looking at college classes."

"That is great," Jonah said. "But—isn't JB worried about messing up time? Doesn't that throw things off, with the way the twenty-first century is supposed to go?"

On the computer screen, Daniella shrugged.

"No one *here* was worried about that," she said. "But JB's on his way over to talk to you about it."

"To me?" Jonah repeated.

Just then the door opened, and JB stepped into the room. Jonah left the Skype conversation and went over to talk to the time agent.

"You're using doors now?" Jonah joked. "No more just appearing out of thin air?"

"Nobody can zap themselves in and out of this room," JB explained. "We've got it set up as a dead zone in time. To protect you and Gavin. Because—"

"Because you haven't caught Gary and Hodge yet," Jonah finished for him.

Jonah had been out of bed for a while, and though he was getting better, he still got dizzy easily. He leaned against the wall and then, a moment later, slid down to sit on the floor.

JB sat down beside him.

"We're trying," JB said.

"Why wasn't the time prison a dead zone in time?" Jonah asked. "Why wasn't it a place that nobody could zap in or out of? Why did you let Gary and Hodge escape in the first place?"

"Jonah, we didn't think they could," JB said. "It's complicated, but we're trying as hard as we can to find them and lock them away for good. And to figure out how to make sure they can't ever escape again, this time around."

Jonah pressed down on the edge of a piece of bandage tape that had come undone on his right ankle. It held down the gauze covering one of his two bullet wounds.

"JB, when all this started, I thought you and the other time agents knew everything," Jonah said. "Remember how upset you were just because you thought Angela was supposed to marry a plumber and have five kids? And time travelers messed that up?"

"We see the early twenty-first century differently now,"

JB admitted. "Our attitude before was that every part of the past was set in concrete. But now . . ."

"What?" Jonah asked. "Now it's quicksand?"

JB didn't laugh the way Jonah wanted him to.

"One of our greatest time experts just made that same analogy," JB said. "I prefer to use the word 'malleable.' Some parts of the past are malleable. It's almost like they're begging to be changed."

This reminded Jonah of something Gavin had said back in 1918 about giving the toy soldiers to Leonid: *It's not like I changed things, exactly. It's more like I fixed things to the way they should have gone. It's like . . . improving on original time. Like time itself wants something different. Don't you feel it? I think those are the only things you can do anything about.*

How could there be some things that were supposed to be changed, and some things that were dangerous to change? How was anyone supposed to know the difference?

"It's like we're back to talking about fate," Jonah complained. "Why don't you just tell me everything I'm supposed to do, and I'll just do it, and that'll be that?"

"Because that's too much of a difference," JB said. "That's just you obeying orders, not making up your own mind. That's you being trapped."

And I'm not already trapped? Jonah wondered. *When I can't* leave this hospital room and I've been shot and so much that happened to me in the past few months was totally out of my control?

But he could also think of moments—even moments in 1918—when he'd taken matters into his own hands. When he'd done something to be proud of.

So why couldn't I have figured out a way to save all the Romanovs? Jonah wondered.

He sighed. He really didn't feel well enough yet to think about all of that, or to discuss it with JB.

"Okay," Jonah said. "We won't go into any of that. But if you won't tell me my future, then tell me my past. Tell me which famous missing kid of history I used to be."

"Jonah," JB groaned. "You know I can't do that. You know your past is too closely connected to your future."

"You mean because I still have to go back to my original time," Jonah said quietly, trying to hold back the fear in his voice.

"Well . . .," JB began, his eyes darting around. "Right now I can tell you—"

"Never mind," Jonah said quickly. How could JB be hedging even on this, when Jonah already knew it was true?

Jonah looked across the room, to where Gavin was still chatting with Daniella by computer. They seemed to be exchanging jokes—Russian jokes.

Actually, it sounds like they're reminding each other about jokes their father told them when they were growing up in the early 1900s, Jonah realized. *Which is why they're both crying and laughing, all at once.*

"I started looking for my identity on my own," Jonah said defiantly, glancing back at JB. "Back home, with Katherine. And then here, last night when I couldn't sleep. . . ."

"But you didn't find anything, did you?" JB asked.

Jonah knew that JB would have made a lot of information off-limits on the hospital computer. But was he keeping information away from Jonah that he would have had access to in the twenty-first century?

"When I go back home, you can't control my computer there," Jonah said.

An awful thought struck him.

"Katherine and I didn't set everything in motion, did we?" Jonah asked. "We were looking up the Romanovs, and then Daniella was on our front porch, and a few minutes later Gavin was kidnapping all of us . . ."

JB looked startled.

"I don't *think* so," he said. "I think there's still room for total coincidences. . . . But maybe we've been wrong about that, too."

JB seemed so rattled by this thought that Jonah almost felt sorry for him.

Jonah shook his hair back from his face. It was getting a little too long—he'd have to have it cut before he actually went home. Or else that alone would tip off Mom and Dad that something very strange had happened, that Jonah had been away from home for more than just an instant.

And could that mess up time?

Could it mess up Jonah's fate?

"The whole thought of destiny and fate makes my head hurt," Jonah complained to JB. "After we came back from 1903, you were saying it would be God who determined that. But this time around, in 1918, who died? Who survived? The only people who lived were the ones Gary and Hodge picked. It's kind of like Leonid and Maria owe their lives to Gary and Hodge just as much as they owe Katherine."

"You don't think good can come out of bad?" JB asked. "That bad people can't do bad things and have there be some good results too?"

He sounded more confident, making that argument.

"I guess none of us missing children from history would have lived, period, if it hadn't been for Gary and Hodge kidnapping us way back at the beginning of all this," Jonah said. He peeked toward JB, hoping his expression would give away an answer—and maybe some sort of indication about Jonah's original fate.

JB stayed poker-faced.

"And that's why Gavin thought he should work for Gary and Hodge in the first place," Jonah continued.

"He's not working for them anymore," JB said.

"I know," Jonah said. "But things did change because of him. I mean, just think about what he saw on the Internet the one day, and then what Katherine and I saw the next . . . and then what actually happened . . ."

JB nodded grimly.

"We're still trying to figure out how all that worked," JB said. "How could Gavin and Gary and Hodge have caused such dramatic changes so quickly without ruining everything else? We have to face up to the possibility that Gary and Hodge might have better technology than we do, or that they figured out something in time prison that we don't know."

Jonah didn't want to think about Gary and Hodge having any advantages. He looked away. Across the room, the basketball had started to roll slowly toward him—probably proving that the floor wasn't perfectly level. Jonah hadn't noticed that before.

Were there things like that in time travel, things that only showed up when you made your observations over a very long time? And then lived through lots of changes?

Jonah sighed.

"I've had a lot of time to think in here," he said. "It's like, people use the word 'fate' just to label a lot of things we don't understand. But I still don't understand. Just look at, I don't know, Alexei and Anastasia's sisters. Why was it Maria's fate to live, but Tatiana's and Olga's fate to die?"

"I don't know," JB said quietly. "But I'm feeling more and more certain that there must have been a reason. It's just not something we're going to understand anytime soon."

That didn't help.

"But you knew that some of the Romanovs had to die, didn't you?" Jonah asked. "Even when Katherine thought she was going back to save all of them . . . it really wasn't possible, was it?"

"'Possible'?" JB repeated. "I've seen a lot of things happen that I didn't think were possible before I met you and Katherine."

This was such an unsatisfactory answer that Jonah could only glare at JB. After a few moments, JB gave a helpless shrug and shook his head.

"You're right—I don't think there's any way the tsar could have survived without throwing history off track," he said. "Without causing time itself to collapse. And if Katherine had managed to save everyone but him, that would have been too much of a change too. But I'm not entirely sure where the tipping point was. It would seem that saving Chip, Leonid, and the three youngest Romanovs was the best we could hope for."

Jonah clenched and unclenched his fists.

"But you took such a risk with Katherine's life," Jonah said. "You knew what she would do when you put the Elucidator on the table, didn't you? And you knew there was a chance she wouldn't even be invisible anymore, going back to 1918 . . ."

Somehow Jonah was angrier about JB endangering Katherine's life than he'd ever been about any risks to his own life.

JB rubbed his hand against his forehead.

"Of course I knew what Katherine would do, given the opportunity," JB said. "I've seen the two of you in action in five different centuries, not to mention several random time hollows. Putting that Elucidator down in front of her was one of the hardest things I've ever made myself do. But I thought we all owed it to Chip and the others—and I knew she thought so too. And . . ."

"And what?" Jonah challenged.

"And I trusted her," JB said simply. "I had faith that she'd do everything she could."

But she's my sister, Jonah wanted to scream. *And she could have died.*

But how could he, when protecting Katherine would

have meant condemning five other kids to die?

Jonah didn't say anything, and for a long moment JB didn't either. Then JB put his hand on Jonah's shoulder.

"I can tell you one thing," JB said. "We've thoroughly checked out the aftermath of 1918, and there's no problem with Gavin and Daniella and Maria being saved. That night in the cellar, the guards were too drunk and disturbed to actually count the bodies. And then it looks like Gary and Hodge faked the remains after that convincingly enough. People will know the truth by *my* time period, but by then it won't matter."

"What about Leonid?" Jonah asked.

JB shook his head.

"His situation was a bit more worrisome, because he was supposed to live into the 1920s," JB said. "But everything's all right with him now too."

So everything's fixed for the ones who lived, Jonah thought. *The others are being kept alive in the survivors' memories. Is that enough?*

JB started to stand up.

"I've got to go," he said. "We're kind of short-staffed right now, because we have so many people out looking for Gary and Hodge and trying to protect the missing kids they kidnapped. They needed me on duty five minutes ago."

Jonah wasn't going to let this bit of news get past him.

"You mean, all the kidnapped kids are in danger?" Jonah asked. "Even people like Andrea and Emily and Alex who lived out their pasts already?"

JB put his hands on Jonah's shoulders.

"Don't worry about it," JB said. "We've got guards posted with everyone, whether they know it or not. Everything's under control."

He gave Jonah one last pat on the shoulders and then went back out the door.

Jonah did not feel comforted.

He looked up and saw that Gavin was watching him. The other boy had finished his Skype conversation and closed the laptop.

"Daniella had an idea," Gavin said. "She thinks I should transfer to your school."

Jonah blinked.

"You mean, back home?" he asked. "You want to go to Harris Middle School?"

"Daniella's starting there new, so why shouldn't I?" Gavin asked.

"Well, because . . . your family didn't move, did they?" Jonah asked.

"No, but I can do some kind of in-district transfer," Gavin said. "My, um, my mom was trying to talk me into something like that right before we all went back to 1918."

Jonah squinted at Gavin. It was hard to get his brain to adjust to thinking about middle school, not about the big topics like life and death and fate and danger. But Gavin acted like Jonah's silence was a question.

"All right, all right, I'll tell you why," Gavin said. "I kind of . . . got in with a bad crowd in my regular school. You remember those kids I was hanging out with at the adoption conference?"

"In the matching skull sweatshirts," Jonah said. "The kids who were mean to Katherine and me."

"Yeah," Gavin said, sounding embarrassed. "Those were my friends. Most of them aren't even adopted. They were just . . ."

"Making trouble," Jonah said.

Gavin nodded.

"And I get in trouble when I hang out with them," he admitted. "But if I switched to Harris Middle School . . . well, you and Chip and Katherine and Daniella would hang out with me, wouldn't you?"

For a minute Jonah was afraid Gavin would even ask, *You'd be my friend, wouldn't you?* Which would have been really weird. Jonah had gone back to 1918 with Gavin and seen him on the verge of death and been willing to risk his own life to save his. But there were some lines that just shouldn't be crossed.

"Sure," Jonah said quickly, before Gavin went any

further. "I'd hang out with you. Maybe you could even try out for basketball with Chip and me."

Instantly Jonah recognized his mistake.

"I'm sorry, I'm sorry! I guess that wouldn't work with your hemophilia, would it?" Jonah asked.

Gavin lifted his head.

"Maybe it could," he said. "Maybe this is the bargain I need to make with my mom. I switch schools and stop hanging out with juvenile delinquents; she stops babying me so much; I promise to always do my injections on game days. . . . We can work things out."

Gavin looked so pleased, Jonah almost felt bad telling him the truth. But he had to.

"Gavin, it's not like Chip and me . . . well, we're not the popular kids at Harris," Jonah said. "Nobody really knows or cares who we are. I mean, *I* don't even know who I am! Or who I *was* in history . . ."

Gavin shook his head.

"Jonah, of course you know who you are," he said. "You're the one everyone trusts. You're the one who tried and tried and tried to save my family, even when Chip and Katherine were ready to give up. You're the one who wanted to save my life even after I put your life in danger. Doesn't that matter more than knowing a name from the past?"

If Jonah had thought it would have been awkward and

embarrassing to hear Gavin ask, *You'd be my friend, wouldn't you?* then this was almost worse.

"But what if . . ." Jonah stopped. He thought about what he was going to say, then went ahead. If Gavin was going to be so blindingly earnest, then Jonah could do that too. "What if, when it's my turn, in my own time period, I'm not that person? What if I fail when it comes time to live out my own part of history?"

Gavin stood up and walked unsteadily toward Jonah, just to punch him in the arm.

"Then you can count on the rest of us to help you," he said. "We've got your back! You'll be fine!"

Jonah knew that Gavin was sincere. He knew that Gavin wanted to make up for everything he'd done wrong. But Gavin had only gone back in time to one dangerous time period. Jonah had centuries more experience than that. Jonah felt like an old man listening to a little kid tell him that everything was going to work out great.

Is this how all those old time-travel experts felt listening to Katherine argue for saving the Romanovs? Jonah wondered. *But—she was right! Sort of. At least, she managed to save some of them.*

"Uh, thanks," Jonah told Gavin. And then, because he didn't want to talk about anything else right now, he added, "Want to go back to playing basketball?"

Gavin shrugged and nodded, and Jonah picked up the ball. But the game had changed. This time, with every thud of the ball against the floor, Jonah felt time passing, time zooming forward.

And all of that time was bringing Jonah closer and closer to his own fate.

AUTHOR'S NOTE

When I started writing the Missing series in early 2007, it seemed like a no-brainer to include Alexei Romanov and Anastasia Romanova as two of the famous missing children from history. As the only son and youngest daughter of the last tsar of Russia, they'd led fascinating and tragic lives. I knew it was likely that they'd died with the rest of their family on July 17, 1918, but as of early 2007—even after nearly ninety years—there was still enough evidence missing that it seemed possible at least one Romanov might have survived that gruesome night.

But our knowledge of history can change dramatically even without time travel. And even ninety years is not long enough to be sure that all the evidence is in. New discoveries in the summer of 2007 and new revelations in 2009 eliminated virtually all doubt about what really happened to the youngest Romanovs.

Since I'd already mentioned the Romanov kids in *Found*, I decided to keep them in the series regardless. I reasoned that if people from the future had mastered time travel, they could also master faking human remains well enough to trick twenty-first-century DNA tests.

In reality, the Romanov mystery has been solved. But it's still a fascinating story.

Alexei and Anastasia were part of a family that began ruling Russia in 1613. Their father, Nicholas II, became tsar when his own father, Alexander III, died suddenly in 1894. Nicholas II was largely unprepared to lead such a vast country, and his shy, mild-mannered personality was hardly suited to the role of an autocratic monarch. His wife, Alexandra, was more forceful—and she was fully convinced that Nicholas had the divine right to rule. But the Russians generally disliked her because she was viewed as an outsider, a German princess meddling in Russian affairs.

The birth of Nicholas and Alexandra's children complicated matters even more.

In the Russian system, only a male could inherit the throne. So when Nicholas and Alexandra began by having four daughters—Olga in 1895, Tatiana in 1897, Maria in 1899, and Anastasia in 1901—it just set everyone up to be that much more thrilled when Alexei was born in 1904. His birth was welcomed with a 301-gun salute in St. Petersburg and the pealing of church bells across the country.

But the family's excitement soon turned to worry, sorrow, and fear.

When Alexei was only six weeks old, he started bleeding from the navel, the first sign of his hemophilia.

Hemophilia is a hereditary condition, and it had entered the royal families of not just Russia but also Germany and Spain through the female descendants of Queen Victoria of the United Kingdom. Alexandra, Alexei's mother, had unknowingly been a carrier.

The treatment of hemophilia has changed immensely over the past century, as scientists have figured out ways to compensate for the blood's inability to clot. The same week I started writing this author's note, scientists announced very promising results of gene-therapy tests that enhanced clotting ability for people with hemophilia for more than a year.

But in the early 1900s, little could be done for Alexei, aside from trying to keep him from getting any cut, scrape, or bruise. This, of course, was impossible to prevent completely, and Alexei spent much of his childhood in pain. Even the most minor bump could lead to burst veins and arteries that bled into his joints, causing great agony and sometimes weeks of not being able to walk. And with each bleed there was the possibility that this would be the one that didn't stop—the one that would kill him.

Nicholas and Alexandra learned the truth about Alexei's condition early on, but they were determined to keep it secret from their subjects. They didn't want any hint that Alexei might not be able to rule, or that he might not live long enough to take the throne. As Alexei grew up, many Russians must have known that something was wrong, especially when Alexei was seen being carried, even at ceremonial occasions. But such public appearances were limited. Alexandra already wanted to protect her children from what she perceived as decadent Russian society; Alexei's illness made her withdraw her children from public view and from social interaction all the more.

Alexei's condition also made Nicholas and Alexandra dependent on the one man who seemed to be able to help Alexei: Grigori Rasputin, who was, depending on your viewpoint, either a mystic healer and a holy man, or a religious fake. Some speculate that Rasputin had such a hypnotic effect on Alexei that, even in the midst of a serious bleed, Alexei would calm down enough that the bleeding would stop. But the Russian nobility blamed Rasputin for many of the country's problems, and a group of them ended up assassinating him in 1916. (Contributing to the notion that Rasputin did have special powers, he supposedly survived being knifed, poisoned, shot, and beaten before his assassins finally succeeded in drowning him.)

If you look at the pictures of the Romanov children growing up—and there are lots and lots of those pictures, because the whole family loved cameras—it's easy to forget that they lived in turbulent times, and that more and more people outside the palace walls were coming to believe that the rule of the tsars had to end. For the five Romanov kids, their lives were an odd mix of being very privileged, very sheltered, and in some ways very restricted. Their family owned seven palaces, and the girls each received a diamond and a pearl every year on their birthdays, with the idea that they would have enough for a full necklace of each by the time they were sixteen. But both of their parents preferred a simpler lifestyle than many people would have chosen given their incredible wealth and power. Even when their father was still in power, the children grew up taking cold baths and sleeping on simple camp-style cots with no pillows.

Strangely, the way the Romanov kids were raised turned out to be fairly good preparation for their last months of imprisonment. Theirs was a close-knit family, and as children they had mostly played only with one another. So being trapped with just their parents and siblings and a few servants probably didn't seem as devastating to them as it might have for kids who were used to being around a lot of friends.

Still, for most of their lives, the Romanov children were protected from the unrest outside their palace walls. A great deal changed with the start of World War I in 1914. In early 1915, the tsar left Tsarskoe Selo, the family's eight-hundred-acre palace compound near St. Petersburg, to take command of the military forces at headquarters near the front hundreds of miles away. To Alexei's great delight, he was allowed to go live with his father at headquarters later that same year. The eleven-year-old boy, who had always been so protected and babied, was delighted to get the chance to live more roughly and be around soldiers and learn everything he could about the military. However, this glorious freedom ended for him about a year later, after a massive nosebleed and other hemophilia-related problems forced him to return home.

Meanwhile, the tsarina and her four daughters considered it their patriotic duty to help wounded soldiers. Alexandra, Olga, and Tatiana all went through nursing programs. Maria and Anastasia were not old enough to be trained as nurses, but they visited the military hospitals as well. All of the Romanov females were exposed to grisly sights, and the tsarina made it clear that she and her daughters would pitch in and help no matter how much filth and blood and gore they encountered.

Russia entered World War I with plenty of fervor and nationalistic pride, but it quickly became clear that the country's military was woefully unprepared. After a series of humiliating losses and a mounting death count, the mood of the country began to turn. The grief and resentment of families who'd lost sons and husbands fed into the calls for revolution. A February 1917 demonstration calling for "bread and peace" turned into violent riots in St. Petersburg, with thousands of soldiers turning against the government as well. The capital was in chaos. Even the tsar himself came to believe that the only way to end the unrest was for him to step down.

Ultimately, Tsar Nicholas II abdicated his throne on March 15, 1917. Not wanting to endanger his sickly son, the tsar indicated that his brother Michael—not Alexei— should take the throne in his place. But just trading one tsar for another was not enough for the revolutionaries. Michael never actually took over, and he ended up being murdered a month before his brother.

At first the royal rule was replaced by a provisional government led by Alexander Kerensky, who had been a parliamentary leader during Nicholas II's reign. But the more extreme Bolsheviks overthrew this government and took over in October 1917.

At the time of the tsar's abdication, all five of his children had the measles—so badly that they had to have their heads shaved. Anastasia and Tatiana also had burst eardrums because of the measles and so were temporarily deaf. Their mother couldn't even tell them what had happened—she had to write it down for them.

If the five Romanov offspring had been well enough to travel, and if their parents had chosen to act immediately, they probably could have left the country right away and moved to England, where a cousin, George V, was on the throne. The British government made a formal offer of asylum on March 22. But then the British backed away from that offer. Among other issues, the British leaders worried about Alexandra's German connections, since Britain was still in the midst of fighting Germany in World War I.

The British also may not have fully understood that the Romanovs' lives were in danger.

At first the family was simply kept under house arrest at Tsarskoe Selo. Then in August 1917 they were sent to western Siberia, to a place called Tobolsk. After the Bolsheviks took over, they were moved again. When they were taken from Tobolsk to Ekaterinburg, in the heart of revolutionary territory, they had to have known it was a bad sign.

Alexei was once again very ill, and so Nicholas, Alexandra, and Maria went to Ekaterinburg first, and were joined by the others about a month later.

In Ekaterinburg, the Romanovs moved into a house that had been taken away from a retired engineer named Nikolai Ipatiev. The Bolsheviks referred to it rather chillingly as the House of Special Purpose—the "special purpose" never actually being spelled out. Ipatiev's house was large and well-furnished, but the seven Romanovs, their four servants, and the doctor were crowded into five rooms. And the double fences, armed guards, and blocked windows were constant reminders that the Romanovs were imprisoned there. At one point Anastasia tried to peek out a window, and a guard immediately began firing toward her. (Most versions of this story I encountered said this happened to either Anastasia or "one of the sisters"; one version claimed it was the tsar himself who was fired upon. Anastasia seems the likeliest person to show such curiosity and risk-taking; regardless, the guards made it clear that that wasn't allowed.)

Surprisingly, the Romanovs were allowed to keep some of their valuables, such as imperial bed linens and tableware. And the original commander and guards at Ekaterinburg didn't treat the family too badly. When Yakov Yurovsky took over as commander in early July and brought in new guards, they took a more hardcore approach.

The Romanovs' captors were afraid that some of the family's loyal friends would try to free them. A few notes were smuggled in with food deliveries—hidden in loaves of bread or, in one case, wrapped around the cork stopper of a bottle of cream—asking about the family's condition and the possibilities for escape and/or rescue. The family responded to the notes with caution, apparently because they couldn't be sure if the notes were real and not fakes set up to catch them plotting against the government.

Either way, nothing came of the notes in the end. According to writings the Romanovs left behind and the descriptions of their captors, the family mostly seemed to accept their imprisonment with unusual calm, taking refuge in their religious beliefs and a regular routine of family meals, morning and afternoon walks, and evening card-playing and reading.

Meanwhile, with fighting in the mountains near Ekaterinburg, the Romanovs' captors knew the city was about to be retaken from the revolutionaries, and they feared the Romanovs might be freed that way. It's unclear how much of the decision to kill the Romanovs was made by local officials and how much was dictated by the national leadership. The local officials did send a telegram to Moscow on July 16 saying they couldn't wait, but they didn't send it until late in the day. And because of disruptions in the telegraph lines, the message didn't arrive until hours after that. There's no official record of a reply, but Yurovsky later claimed that he had received an order from Moscow.

Regardless, Yurovsky's plans went just as they're described in this book (at least just as they're described apart from the time travelers' changes). Yurovsky did send away the kitchen boy, Leonid Sednev, on July 16, since he didn't want to kill the boy with everyone else. However, his excuse about the boy visiting his uncle was a lie, since the uncle had already been murdered by the Bolsheviks. In reality, Leonid spent the night across the street in a house where the external guards slept—and where he undoubtedly could hear the shots fired at the Romanovs. He became the only Ipatiev House servant to survive that night.

It was about one thirty a.m. when Yurovsky woke Dr. Botkin to tell him that the fighting was getting too close and the family had to be moved. The family did take about forty-five minutes to get ready, probably because they were debating about what they should take with them and what they would need to leave behind. The seven Romanovs, Dr. Botkin, and the three remaining servants did rather cluelessly follow the guards down to the cellar.

Yurovsky kept the whole group waiting in the cellar for another half an hour, while he made sure that the truck arrived and everything was prepared. Alexandra really did demand chairs for her and Alexei, and the guards provided them.

According to Yurovsky, the family seemed stunned when he read off the charges against the former tsar.

Accounts vary about exactly what Yurovsky said: Did he talk about the nearby fighting and efforts to rescue the Romanovs? Or the fact that their relatives in Europe fought against Russia? Or did he focus more on what one account called the former tsar's "countless bloody crimes" against the Russian people? (I included all three issues in the charges I depicted Yurovsky reading in *Risked*.) Yurovsky claims he himself took the first shot at the tsar, and then a team of assassins all began shooting at once. Reportedly, none of the guards actually wanted to kill the girls, but theirs became particularly horrific deaths, probably because of the jewels sewn into their clothing and the assassins' disorganization and poor planning. When the four girls—and the maid, the doctor, and even Alexei— were still alive even after the extreme barrage of bullets, the assassins resorted to shooting them point-blank in the head and/or using bayonets to stab them to death.

Just as the killings were botched, so were the attempts to hide the bodies afterward. Yurovsky had planned to dump all the bodies down a deserted mine shaft in an uninhabited area outside the city. But the truck broke down and got stuck in mud, and Yurovsky's men were forced to move the bodies part of the way in carts. They encountered peasants preparing to mow hay, and Yurovsky had to send men into a nearby village to tell people to stay out of the area—so much for the idea of secrecy. Then when the men dropped the bodies into the mine shaft, the water at the bottom proved to be too shallow to cover them. The men threw grenades down into the shaft, hoping to collapse the walls onto the bodies, but this failed too.

With the sun already up by then, Yurovsky realized he'd just need to leave guards near the mine shaft and come back later to move the bodies again.

More car and truck problems and a series of injuries complicated Yurovsky's second night of trying to hide the bodies elsewhere. He resorted to doing his best to disguise the bodies so that even if they were found they wouldn't be recognized. His men threw sulfuric acid into a collective grave they dug, and this ate away at the corpses. Also, Yurovsky later wrote, he had his men separate two of the bodies from the rest so the men could burn them and bury them elsewhere. He reasoned that anyone finding just nine bodies would not automatically know that it was the Romanovs and their servants.

The official story about the killings that went out on July 20—just five days before Ekaterinburg did indeed fall to the army that would have rescued the Romanovs—was that only the former tsar had been killed; the rest of the family was said to be alive and well and in a hidden location.

That original lie fed rumors later on that at least one

of the Romanovs had somehow escaped. As the years passed, a variety of pretenders cropped up claiming to be Romanovs. The most attention went to a woman named Anna Anderson, who turned up in Germany in 1920 and managed to convince many people—including some Romanov relatives—that she really was Anastasia. Multiple authors wrote books that advanced or discredited her story; a TV movie based on her life billed her as "the great romantic enigma of the twentieth century."

When Anna Anderson died in 1984, it seemed that she had carried her secrets to the grave. However, DNA tests done ten years later proved conclusively that Anna Anderson could not have been Anastasia.

The actual whereabouts of the Romanovs' bodies remained secret—at least publicly—during most of the history of the Soviet Union. An amateur historian and a filmmaker found some of the bodies in the 1970s, but they didn't feel it was safe to reveal their discovery for another decade. In 1991 the skeletal remains were finally dug up and studied and analyzed, and scientists determined that they belonged to Nicholas, Alexandra, and three of their daughters, along with the three servants and Dr. Botkin.

Alexei's body was missing, and so was one sister's, although scientists disagreed about whether it was Anastasia or Maria.

For a while, the two missing bodies fueled even more speculation. But then, sixteen years later, remains of two more bodies were found nearby. These remains were broken and burned, fitting with the claim that Yurovsky and his men had unsuccessfully tried to cremate two of the bodies before burying them.

According to scientists, the DNA tests on those remains were conclusive: They belonged to the missing Romanov children. In real history, there was never any hope for any of the Romanovs from the moment they stepped into that cellar in the middle of the night on July 17, 1918.

But what does it say about human nature that so many people wanted to believe, so desperately, for so many years, that at least one of the children had lived?

ACKNOWLEDGMENTS

Volumes have been written about the Romanovs and their horrific deaths. I am grateful to all the researchers, scientists, writers, and translators who have worked to ferret out the truth and share it with the rest of the world. Given what is known now, I found it a little amusing that so many of the books published before 2007 claimed to "prove" implausible scenarios to account for the missing bodies. But many of those older books were useful for background information and eyewitness accounts. I greatly appreciated the 2008 book *The Last Days of the Romanovs: Tragedy at Ekaterinaburg* by Helen Rappaport, because it provided newer information and focused so precisely on the Romanovs' time at the Ipatiev House. For a broader overview of the Romanovs' lives (and for its many, many pictures), I also appreciated *Tsar: The Lost World of Nicholas and Alexandra* by Peter Kirth.

Useful resources I found online included http://www.romanov-memorial.com/, which has detailed blueprints and pictures of the Ipatiev House. It was also helpful (though unsettling) to read the eyewitness accounts from Yurovsky and some of the other assassins online at http://www.kingandwilson.com/FOTRresources/.

In addition to the books and online resources I used for

research, I am also very grateful to Rob Alexander, executive director of the Central Ohio chapter of the National Hemophilia Foundation, for answering my questions about what Gavin's experiences with hemophilia would be like in the modern world.

ABOUT THE AUTHOR

MARGARET PETERSON HADDIX is the author of many critically and popularly acclaimed teen and middle-grade novels, including The Missing series, the Shadow Children series, *Claim to Fame*, *Palace of Mirrors*, and *Uprising*. A graduate of Miami University (of Ohio), she worked for several years as a reporter for the *Indianapolis News*. She also taught at Danville (Illinois) Area Community College. She lives with her family in Columbus, Ohio. Visit her at haddixbooks.com.